ROGMASHER RAMPAGE

BILLY CLIKK

ROGMASHER RAMPAGE

Mark Crilley

Delacorte Press

This book is dedicated to
Tetsu and Kei Hirabayashi
and their families.

Published by
Delacorte Press
an imprint of
Random House Children's Books
a division of Random House, Inc.
New York

Visit us on the Web! www.randomhouse.com/kids
Educators and librarians, for a variety of teaching tools, visit us at
www.randomhouse.com/teachers

Library of Congress Cataloging-in-Publication Data

Crilley, Mark.
Billy Clikk: rogmasher rampage / Mark Crilley.
p. cm.
Summary: Billy's double life—elementary school in Piffling, Indiana, and international monster killer—intensifies as he makes his first solo creatch op in a Chinese mountain village.
ISBN 0-385-73112-4 (trade) — ISBN 0-385-90137-2 (glb)
[1. Monsters—Fiction. 2. Villages—Fiction. 3. China—Fiction. 4. Adventure and adventurers—Fiction.] I. Title.
PZ7.C869275Bic 2005
[Fic]—dc22   2005000210

The text of this book is set in 14-point Garamond.

Book design by Jason Zamajtuk

Printed in the United States of America

September 2005

10 9 8 7 6 5 4 3 2 1

BVG

CHAPTER 1

Billy Clikk dug his fingers into the Peruvian murgwod's dorsal fin. This was not easy. The murgwod was soaking wet and covered in mud, and that was on top of the inch-thick layer of slimy exoblubber that coated its entire body. Add to this the fact that Billy was sweating from every pore after a long day trudging through the Peruvian jungle to get to this spot—an area of shallow water at the edge of a muddy branch of the Rio Urubamba—and the conditions for maintaining a good grip on a murgwod were about as poor as they could possibly be.

The murgwod could snap at the air and growl all it wanted. Billy wasn't going anywhere. Billy and his parents, Jim and Linda Clikk, had been charged with finding and neutralizing this creatch, and now that Billy had it in his grasp he wasn't about to let it get away.

As Billy struggled to improve his grip, he surveyed the fearsome beast he was now riding like a bucking bronco: the red, muscular body, the seven-toed feet and their daggerlike claws, the long spiky reptilian tail, the rhino-ish head, the single fiery yellow eye, and the jaws that featured the most ferocious set of incisors Billy had ever seen.

"Got it!" Billy called to his parents, realizing even as he did so that they were unlikely to hear him from where they were, searching in vain for the murgwod more than half a mile up the river. It was just Billy's luck that Orzamo, his half-dog half-lizard friend, was at his parents' side at the moment instead of his. (Billy had actually encouraged her to go help them out, knowing that his parents were pretty tired from a creatch op they'd handled in Norway a day or two earlier.)

No biggie, thought Billy. *Dad let me take on that nine-legged malanoobu by myself last week in Mauritania. How much harder can a murgwod be?*

The murgwod let out a furious growl followed by several defiant grunts, as if it had heard Billy's thoughts and was offended by the comparison. It then launched into an especially vigorous bout of thrashing. Billy dug his heels into the murgwod's ribs, refusing to be thrown.

"Take it easy, pal," Billy said. "I'm just doing my job here."

Just doing his job.

Billy found it useful to treat his bizarre double life—half the time an average sixth grader in Piffling, Indiana, the other half a globe-trotting creach battler for the top-secret monster-containment organization known as AFMEC—as if it were no big deal. If he stopped and thought about it for too long it would probably drive him nuts. In fact, pretty much every aspect of his life now required putting certain thoughts out of his head as he focused on the task at hand. This Peruvian murg-wod, for instance. If Billy allowed himself to dwell on the fact that this particular murgwod had been terrorizing villagers up and down the Rio Urubamba for the past three weeks, swallowing their chickens and pigs whole and, on occasion, leaving men and women with missing limbs and hideous scars . . . well, he'd be a lot better off *not* dwelling on it. So he didn't.

"All right," said Billy, panting loudly as he prepared to take things to the next level. "Just work with me here and you'll make things a lot easier for both of us."

Billy knew the standard procedure for dealing with a murg-wod. He'd studied all the steps just a few months earlier, preparing for his first round of AFMEC entrance exams, and had gone back to the *Sea Creatch Guidebook* to memorize them word for word while gearing up for the current creach op. He also knew that every step in the murgwod subduing procedure ("Grasp the dorsal fin firmly with both hands while maneuvering your legs into the riding position," "Beware of the murgwod's prehensile tail, an agile fifth limb with a viselike grip") was designed for one purpose and one purpose only: to allow you to knock the creature out with a single shot from a fully loaded Skump pistol, expertly fired into the cranial artery: a half-inch-wide blood vessel tucked just beneath a fold of skin at the base of the murgwod's neck.

Billy was right where he needed to be to fire that shot, and no doubt the murgwod's cranial artery was where it needed to be to receive it, but Billy's Skump pistol—the one he'd used just moments before to force the murgwod out of hiding—was buried in the mud on the shore behind him. He'd chucked it there when he realized he'd run out of ammo.

Good thing I brought a klimper dart with me.

Billy wiped the sweat from his eyes for the umpteenth time that afternoon, reached down, and pulled the dart container out of his back pocket. He wished that his Affy friend Ana García could be there to see him as he snapped it open with his left hand while maintaining his grip on the murgwod's fin with his right. She was the one who had taught him how to open a klimper dart case with one hand. She was also the one who had thought he was crazy when he proceeded to practice doing it for hours on end, first with one hand, then the other. ("*Next thing you'll be opening one with your feet,"* she'd said with a laugh. Billy had been too embarrassed to admit he'd already been working on that. And had become pretty good at it, as a matter of fact.)

No second chances with this sucker, Billy reminded himself as he raised the klimper dart into the air and prepared to jab it into the murgwod's neck. Klimper darts were nearly as effective as Skump pistols, but they contained only a single payload of klimp toxin. *One inch too far to the left or right and this dart will be about as deadly as a big fat kiss on the lips.*

Billy watched and waited, remembering the words he'd memorized the night before from the guidebook: "The murgwod's cranial artery reveals itself once every eleven seconds, raising the skin at the base of the neck by a mere fraction of an inch as blood courses through it. The well-trained Affy will take notice of this momentary irregularity in the surface of the skin as he aims and fires his Skump pistol into the artery at point-blank range."

Point-blank was out of the question. If Billy hoped to have even half a chance of piercing the murgwod's leathery skin, he'd have to raise the klimper dart over his head and bring it down with all the force he could deliver.

The murgwod let out a vicious growl and shook Billy so hard he almost fell off. Billy had to mash his whole body down against the murgwod's back just to stay put. Making an accurate klimper dart stab under these conditions seemed next to impossible.

I can do this. Just have to stay focused. Put everything else out of my mind.

The murgwod slowed its thrashing for a moment. Billy sat up straight again, breathed deeply, and held the dart just above the murgwod's neck before raising it into position high in the air.

One shot. That's all I need.

Billy kept his eyes trained on the skin at the base of the murgwod's neck, watching, waiting. The murgwod lurched violently back and forth. Dollops of its exoblubber pelted Billy in the face.

Then he saw it: the skin swelling as blood coursed through the cranial artery. *Bingo!*

But just as Billy was preparing to deliver the crucial blow, the murgwod ceased its thrashing, took hold of Billy with its tail, and dove headfirst into the river. Billy lost all sense of balance as he went entirely underwater. He'd barely had a chance to hold his breath before he went under, and for a moment he feared the worst: that the murgwod would just go to the bottom of the river and hold him there. But no. It had other plans.

The murgwod resurfaced long enough for Billy to see where

it was taking him: downstream, to a spot where the river descended into a treacherous patch of rocks and rapids.

Urubamba rapids, thought Billy. *I can handle that.* A lifetime of extreme sports—including a near suicidal entry in Lunatic Louie's Whitewater Madness rafting competition a year or two earlier (in which he'd bagged first prize)—had prepared Billy for the sort of risks that would have most kids his age wetting their pants.

Even Billy had his limits, though. And when he took a moment to consider what lay *beyond* Urubamba rapids, he realized that all the extreme sports in the world wouldn't be enough to bail him out this time.

The falls, thought Billy. *It's heading for the falls!*

Urubamba Falls. A one-hundred-foot sheer drop to pounding water and jagged rocks. If Billy went over, the chances for survival were virtually nil. Murgwods, with their hard skin and flexible bones, were pretty much designed for going over waterfalls and sailing through without a scratch. Sixth graders like Billy Clikk were designed for going over waterfalls and breaking every single bone in their entire bodies.

Billy tried to come up with a plan as the two of them plunged underwater again, his already aching limbs struggling to maintain a good grip on the dorsal fin. If he let go of it, the murgwod would use its tail to pull him under its belly, depriving him of both air and any means of seeing where they were going.

Maybe I should just pry this tail off me and take my chances trying to escape, he thought. *The murgwod will survive, but so will I.*

It might have been the smart thing to do, but Billy could not consider this as a serious option.

No way. Can't let this murgwod live to terrorize more Peruvians.

The river grew rougher and louder as they entered the rapids. The murgwod darted between the rocks with ease and assurance. How many times had it gone over these falls before? Hundreds? Thousands?

The murgwod surfaced long enough for Billy to catch sight of a battered tree trunk jutting out of the water, just yards from the edge of the falls.

Gotta grab hold of that sucker. It's my only chance.

Billy jammed his klimper dart into his mouth and clenched it between his teeth, freeing up both arms to take hold of the tree trunk. He dug his heels into the murgwod with all his might, causing it to leap up out of the water as it sped toward the falls. Thrusting his arms out as far as he could, he flung them around the tree trunk just as they flew past it.

"Yyyyaaaaggghh!" Pain jolted through Billy's arms as they smashed into the tree trunk, sending splinters flying. It was pure agony, but he held on with all his might. There, no more than five yards in front of them, was the edge of the falls, roaring and churning and threatening to pull Billy and the murgwod over if he lost his grip for even an instant.

The murgwod growled its disapproval. It locked its tail even more tightly around Billy's waist, yanking on him, trying to make him let go and join it in hurtling over the edge of the falls.

No! We are not *going over!*

The water pounded against Billy's thighs and torso, bearing down on him like an endless avalanche. Billy's muscles were tensed to their limits. He knew he wouldn't be able to hold on like this for more than just a few seconds.

Using his tongue and teeth, he maneuvered the klimper dart into position as best he could, then stared at the spot on the murgwod's skin where he'd seen the cranial artery pulse moments before.

No time to wait until it pulses again. I'll have to do it from memory.

Fortunately Billy had noticed a slight discoloration in the skin precisely one inch from where the cranial artery lay.

This is it. Do or die.

Billy pulled his head back as far as he could and slammed

the klimper dart down into the fold of flesh at the base of the murgwod's neck. Even without seeing it, Billy sensed he'd hit the bull's-eye.

GGGRRREEEEEEE-YYYYOOOOGGGHH!

The murgwod let out a piercing scream as it loosened its grip on Billy and drew its lips back into a grimace of pain. It closed its eyes, slipped under the water, and went over Urubamba Falls for the very last time.

CHAPTER 2

Relieved of the murgwod's weight, Billy pulled himself out of the water and up onto the tree trunk. He flopped on top of it, facedown, and decided to stay that way for the rest of the day. He'd have done it too, if his parents and Orzamo hadn't shown up just minutes after he'd sent the murgwod to its watery grave.

"Well done, Billy boy," said Jim Clikk, standing on the shore. "That's two creatches you've defeated single-handedly in just ten days. Something to tell your grandkids about."

"One more creatch like that," said Billy with a cough, "and I'll be lucky if I live long enough to *have* grandkids."

Jim Clikk chuckled knowingly. "You never forget your first murgwod. Never forget the pain, anyway."

"Oh dear," said Linda Clikk as she and Orzamo made their

way across the river to Billy, stepping carefully from one rock to another. "Looks like it cut you up pretty badly with its tail. We'll have to get you back to AFMECopolis right away."

Billy groaned at the thought of repeating the grueling twelve-mile hike they'd made to get to this remote area. "Please tell me they can just send out a flying truck or something to pick us up."

Orzamo bleated her approval of this idea. Her forest creatch skin was suited to northern climes, and the giant Peruvian mosquitos were making a feast out of her.

"No dice, Billy," said Jim. "The Peruvian government had it written into their AFMEC contract that we won't use any trans-gravitational propulsion out here."

Billy sighed. "Isn't there some kind of rule about the Affys who didn't battle the creatch *carrying* the one who did all the way back to camp?" He was joking, but wished it were true all the same.

Linda Clikk put a sympathetic hand on Billy's shoulder. "That's one for you to add to the books when you get elected prime magistrate, dear. How about this, though? Your father and I will divvy up your backpack for the hike back."

Billy pulled himself up to a sitting position and grinned at his mother. "Give me a foot massage and you've got yourself a deal."

Linda Clikk smiled as she smacked Billy right in the middle of his forehead.

"Nice incisions, Clikk," said Mr. Numpler. Billy had successfully dissected his frog well ahead of all the other students in science class, and the teacher wore an expression of mild disbelief. "*Very* nice. Have you . . . *done* this before?"

It was Monday morning, no more than twenty hours after Billy had sent the murgwod over Urubamba Falls. Now he was back at Piffling Elementary, struggling to stay alert after a night that had allowed very little time for sleep. Eighteen of the last twenty hours had been spent outside the United States: nine of them trudging back to camp through the forests of Peru; three of them flying in his parents' gravity-defying BUGZ-B-GON van to AFMEC headquarters; one of them getting bandaged up—and receiving a shot of antibiotics for the murgwod-venom-induced infection—in the AFMECopolis hospital; two of them being debriefed by an overcaffeinated AFMEC paper shuffler named Hossenheffer (who berated Billy for not having rationed his Skump ammo more wisely); and five of them flying back to Piffling, Indiana, where his parents brought the van in for a bumpy landing shortly after dawn, dropping him at their house before rocketing off on a new assignment.

"Nope," said Billy. "First time, Mr. Numpler." And it was

the truth. Billy had never dissected a frog before. He had, however, dissected a twelve-legged klugganork just a few days earlier as part of his Affy entrance exams, and dissecting a frog was pretty much a cinch in comparison. A frog had only a single heart, for one thing. Klugganorks had seven—four of which were hidden in the legs—and if you couldn't pinpoint all of them in under a minute then you could kiss your Affy-in-training status goodbye.

"You've located the liver and the spleen," said Mr. Numpler, tugging his mustache in amazement. "I didn't even *ask* you to locate the liver and the spleen."

"I had time left over," said Billy. "Didn't want to waste it."

"I don't know what's gotten into you this year, Clikk," said Mr. Numpler, "but I like it. Keep up the good work." He gave Billy a suspicious squint and turned his attention to the next student: Kaitlyn Bates, who had hacked her poor frog to pieces without pinpointing much of anything.

Not so long ago Billy was doing well if he could manage Bs and Cs in school. That was before he had discovered that his parents were not pest exterminators (as they had always claimed to be) but agents for AFMEC, the Allied Forces for the Management of Extraterritorial Creatches. It was a top-secret organization whose tireless vigilance protected ordinary men and women from creatches: millions upon millions of horrendous beasts of all shapes and sizes that lurked all over the world, some as vicious and dangerous as murgwods, many much worse. Now that Billy was in on the activities of AFMEC—and even training to be an Affy himself—his Piffling Elementary report card was loaded up with nothing but As. He was being held to a very high standard at AFMEC, and the mental rigors of the job made classes at Piffling El seem like child's play.

It was a cool side effect of his new dual identity, but nothing Billy spent too much time thinking about. He would gladly trade all the good grades in school for an improved score on his last round of Affy entrance exams. There were ten levels all together, and he had only barely made it to the third level. Billy's extreme sports skills had served him well in the "hands-on" tests—those in Introduction to Creatch-Neutralizing Weaponry and Target Practice, and Beginning Transgravitational Propulsion—but he had a long way to go when it came to the written assignments. Even with Ana García's help, his latest essay for Early Twentieth-Century AFMEC History had scored a pitiful thirty-three on the sixty-point AFMEC scale.

"Outlandish," his instructor had written on the first page, just below the title, "Jarrid Glurrik: Alive and Well and Living in Central Europe." Glurrik was the leader of the creatch supremacist movement, a shadowy network of creatches and demi-creatches that sought to destroy AFMEC and take over the earth. Or he *had* been the leader, anyway, until he was killed during a failed attack on AFMEC headquarters in the 1930s. Billy's thesis—that Glurrik's brain had been preserved by creatch supremacists and transplanted into another man's body years later—was admittedly not based on very much in the way of facts.

"Hey, it's *possible,* right?" Billy had said to Ana upon getting his graded paper, errors noted on every page in bright orange ink.

"It's a history class, Billy," Ana had said. "Not a course on paranoid conspiracy theories."

A sudden clattering on the other side of the room—a fallen frog, scalpels and all—snapped Billy back to the here and now of Piffling Elementary. He yawned and checked the clock on the classroom wall. Eleven-forty-five. Five more minutes until lunchtime. Two classes in the afternoon. Then he could get home and hit the sack. There was no telling when the viddy-fone in his back pocket would go off (he had it set to vibrate so as not to blow his cover), signaling the beginning of a new creatch op. He had learned long ago to get sleep whenever he could.

"Yo, Clikkmaster Flash," came an all-too-familiar voice from behind him: Nelson Skubblemeyer, one of the lamest wannabe cool kids in school. With Nelson, everyone was *fill-in-the-blank*-master Flash. He even called Mr. Numpler "Numpmaster Flash." Not to his face, of course. "Help me find this frog's lungs, a'ight? You're, like, down with the science stuff."

"Dude, find your own lungs. I'm not gonna help you cheat."

"Yo. It ain't cheatin'. It's just spreadin' the love, man." Nelson turned his eyes to Billy's hands and forearms, suddenly fascinated by the alarming number of scars and bruises that had accumulated there over the last few months.

"I know you're all freaky *into* this extreme sports thing, but look at yourself. What is *up* with all this? You look like you just stepped out of a zombie flick."

Billy glanced at the scars, each signifying a different creach he had dealt with. The wide gash across the knuckles of his left hand had come to him courtesy of a thorn-clawed voskfursker he'd gotten clobbered by in the wilds of Siberia. The purplish bruise on his right wrist was a memento left by a long-legged bliggit he'd wrestled to the ground somewhere in the outback of western Australia.

"It's this new street luge I'm working on," Billy lied. "Wheels keep coming off."

"Whatevah," said Nelson, rolling his beady eyes. "Now come on, Clikkmaster. Show me the lungs. I *know* you know where they are."

"Look, Nelson, I told you—"

Suddenly, a different voice from behind: "Clikk, you heard the man." Without turning Billy knew who it was: Jake Langley. Jake was, if anything, an even worse wannabe cool kid than Nelson. He wore nothing but black T-shirts day after day and had allowed his curly orange hair to grow into a bushy frizz large and thick enough to house a good-sized rodent. Unlike Nelson, though, Jake was not the sort of kid you could make fun of. A freakish growth spurt had pushed him somewhere near six feet tall, and a steady diet of fast food had him tipping the scales at well over two hundred pounds. Even the toughest jocks in school steered clear of Jake Langley. And it wasn't just his imposing height and weight. It was the crazed look in his eyes.

"Show us the lungs, dude." Billy could smell the barbecue potato chips on Jake's breath. "My boy Nel here is askin' you all polite. What's your problem?"

Nelson Skubblemeyer folded his arms smugly, like a man whose pit bull had just shown up for duty.

Billy wasn't scared of Jake Langley. The hand-to-hand-combat training he'd learned in AFMECopolis was more than enough to leave a thug like Jake unconscious on the science room floor within a matter of seconds. But Billy was under strict orders not to misuse his newly acquired skills. Jake

Langley was irritating and offensive and possessed a body odor that bordered on lethal. He wasn't a creach, though, and as such was off limits.

"Hey, Jake," whispered Billy, "if you're gonna eat potato chips for breakfast, do us all a favor and pop in a few Tic Tacs afterward, will ya?"

Nelson laughed in spite of himself.

Jake Langley's crazed eyes got even crazier. He bared his teeth and stabbed a stubby finger into Billy's chest. "You dissin' me, Clikk? 'Cause I'll beat the snot out of you if you are, you know I will."

"He *will* beat the snot out of you, Clikkmaster," said Nelson, as if acknowledging a sad fact of nature.

Billy tried to stay calm. It would be so easy to challenge

Jake, to tell him they could work this all out, man to man, after school behind the gym. For the sake of his Affy-in-training status, though, he had to defuse the situation. He smiled and raised his hands in a peacemaking gesture. "I'm just messin' with you, Jake. Take it easy."

Jake Langley glared at Billy for a moment, then leaned back in his chair, mercifully taking his body odor with him. "Yeah, well, I ain't messin' with you, Clikk: you got five seconds to show us where those lungs are. And if you don't . . ."

BRREHHHHHHHN!

The blaring school buzzer echoed down the corridors, and in an instant all the students were on their feet, scuffling out of the classroom.

Jake Langley clamped one of his fat hands down on Billy's

shoulder, stopping him from getting up. Nelson looked on, a smirk on his face.

"You're a lucky man, Clikk," said Jake. "Next time you'll do what I tell you to do *when I tell you to do it.* You got that?"

Next time, thought Billy, *I'll treat you to a McKensian neck jab and you'll be unconscious before you even hit the ground.* He knew he'd never do it for real. But that didn't mean he couldn't imagine how good it would feel.

"Whatever you say, Jake," Billy said finally.

"That's better." Jake turned and left the room with Nelson, who looked slightly disappointed that the confrontation hadn't resulted in better fireworks.

Billy reached down to grab his book bag and suddenly felt a pulsing sensation coming from his back pocket. It was his viddy-fone, alerting him to an incoming call from AFMEC.

Another creatch op? Already?

CHAPTER 3

The speed of the viddy-fone's pulse meant the call was urgent. Billy would have to find a way of taking it immediately. He dashed between the rows of half-dissected frogs, flew out the door, and sprinted toward the bathroom.

He got there in record time, but as soon as he pulled the door open, he could hear the voices of at least three boys in the middle of a heated debate about who was the hottest girl in school. It didn't sound like they'd be leaving anytime soon.

The viddy-fone was now pulsing even more insistently. *Can't take the call here. The gym? No. Someone's bound to see me.*

Then it hit him: *the janitor's closet. Perfect!*

Billy tore through the corridors (past two teachers who reminded him not to run in the halls) until he found the dimly lit alcove that housed the janitor's closet. He threw the door open and jumped inside. He flicked on the light switch, pulled the viddy-fone out of his back pocket, and popped it open.

The silver-blue screen crackled to life, snapping into an image of Billy's father, Jim Clikk.

"Hey, Billy. Sorry to call you at school like this but . . ." He stopped midsentence and squinted. "What is that behind your head, a mop?"

"I'm in the janitor's closet."

"Oh. Nice choice."

"What's this about, Dad?"

"The usual, Billy," said Jim Clikk. "Mr. Vriffnee says he's got another creach op with your name on it."

Vriffnee. The prime magistrate of AFMEC. He was tough on all Affys-in-training but had been sending Billy on some especially demanding creach ops. Billy had wondered why Vriffnee was making things hard for him and could come to only one conclusion: Vriffnee had serious doubts about whether Billy had what it took to be a real Affy, and wanted to see if he was worth the trouble—and considerable expense—of training.

Indeed, it was almost as if he wanted Billy to fail and get it over with. In the last month alone Vriffnee had sent Billy up against an array of beasts that seemed calculated to scare him into bailing on his training altogether: a skeletal munkbazzer, a quill-shooting noss lizard, two mammoth sea gribbs (one in the Arctic Circle, another in the Gulf of Bengal), and one saber-clawed desert hurf in an extremely bad mood.

Each creatch op was more difficult and dangerous than the last. Which was just the way Billy liked it. As exhausted as he was from his battle with the murgwod the day before, he was looking forward to whatever Mr. Vriffnee threw at him.

"But, Dad, what about my afternoon classes? You want me to just play hookey?"

"Hookey?" said Jim Clikk with mock horror. Then, smiling: "Basically, yeah. Don't get used to it, though. We don't do things this way very often. Your mother's put a phone call in to the principal's office telling him there's a family emergency."

Billy couldn't help chuckling. In the Clikk family, the word *emergency* took on a whole new meaning.

"What'd you tell them?"

Jim Clikk turned his head to one side and asked someone offscreen a question. "What emergency did you come up with, honey?"

"Aunt Lilly's funeral," said the voice of Linda Clikk.

Billy laughed out loud. "So I have an aunt Lilly now, eh?"

"*Had* an aunt Lilly," said Jim. "So here's the deal. Luigi Bonaducci, an Affy friend of mine, is going to come by the

school in about five minutes, claiming to be a cousin of yours. Just sit tight in the cafeteria until they call you to the office."

"Don't leave me hanging here, Dad. What kind of creatch op is this?"

"What, you want me to spoil the surprise? I'll say this: I sure hope you like kung pao chicken."

China, thought Billy. *Yes!* It was the one country Billy had always wanted to see. And not just for the kung fu and nunchucks either. There was something about China that really captured Billy's imagination. Years earlier there had been a Chinese exchange student at Piffling Elementary, a boy named Shan Ling. Billy had seen a photo album of his and marveled at the temples, the masses of people whizzing around on bicycles, the shop window lettering so complicated it was mind-boggling that anyone was capable of reading it.

"All right, Billy, I'm signing off. Your mother and I are in the middle of something pretty nasty here in Madagascar— dagdoolian wasp-lizards—so we won't be along for the ride." Jim Clikk tried to sound casual as he delivered this news, but Billy knew this was a very big deal. He had never been sent on a creatch op without his parents before.

No way. They're sending me on my first solo creatch op.

"Do us proud, Billy. We'll catch up with you when you get back."

Billy snapped the viddy-fone shut and pumped his fist in the air. "Solo! They're sending me solo! Unbelievable. I must really be advancing through the ranks or something. . . ."

Billy threw the door open and prepared for a mad dash to the cafeteria but found his path neatly blocked by Mr. Coles, the janitor. He was standing there, arms folded over his considerable paunch, a look of suspicion on his puffy red face. Billy stopped dead in his tracks.

"Well, well," said Mr. Coles. "Looks like I found my thief."

Billy watched as Mr. Coles's eyes darted to the closed viddy-fone in Billy's fist, its silver casing too large to hide no matter how tightly Billy closed his fingers around it.

"Th-thief?"

"Somebody made off with my calendar from Mike's Muffler Shop a couple months back, an' now I guess I know just who that someone is."

"It wasn't me," said Billy, somehow sounding guilty in spite of his innocence.

"Oh it wasn't, was it?" Mr. Coles took a step forward, forcing Billy to edge back into the alcove. "Then what is it brings you to my closet here? Lookin' to help me wax the floors after school?"

"I, uh . . ." Billy was at a total loss. Why would he be inside the janitor's closet? There had to be some explanation that sounded reasonable.

"Best confess, boy," said Mr. Coles. His eyes kept darting back to the viddy-fone. "Don't make me drag ya down to the principal's office and name ya as my prime suspect."

"I . . . I needed, um . . ." He shot a glance back at the contents of the closet shelves. There were jugs of detergent, huge cans of floor wax. ". . . I needed to see, uh . . ."

"Needed to see *what?*"

"Needed to see . . . what . . . what kind of rat poison you're using."

Mr. Coles looked genuinely startled. Whatever excuse he'd been expecting, it hadn't been this one. "*Rat* poison?"

"Yeah," said Billy, gaining confidence. "For the rats."

"Get outta here. There ain't no rats in this school."

"Sure there are. In the boys' changing room, just off the gym." Billy had noticed droppings there behind one of the lockers. "I can't believe you let yourself run out of rat poison, Mr. Coles," said Billy, certain that there had never been any rat poison to run out of.

"In the changing room?" Mr. Coles scratched his head, disheveling his thinning gray hair. "You're kidding me."

Billy raised his viddy-fone into plain view and pushed the button that allowed it to double as a business card case.

K'CHIK

He pulled out one of his parents' BUGZ-B-GON business cards and handed it to a now moderately panicked Mr. Coles. "I'd give my folks a call if I were you, Mr. Coles. They deal with rats all the time. And sometimes," Billy added with solemn seriousness, "even things *bigger* than rats."

"Rats in the changing room," said Mr. Coles as Billy dashed off for the cafeteria. "I can't believe it."

CHAPTER 4

Minutes later Billy was called from the cafeteria to the office, where he met for the very first time his "cousin Ralph." Luigi Bonaducci was a huge, hairy guy with hands the size of baseball gloves. He was dressed in a black suit with a black necktie but somehow looked more like a member of a heavy metal band than someone who was heading to a funeral. He had a jagged scar running the length of his neck, which Billy recognized as the handiwork of an iron-tusked moxboarer (one that Billy assumed—judging from Luigi's imposing figure—did not live very long after leaving the scar). He was also pretty old to pass for Billy's cousin, but Penny Hefnik, the school secretary, had clearly bought the story.

"I'm *so* sorry, Billy," she said from behind her desk, her eyebrows crimped in sympathy. "Your mother told me that you were very close to your aunt Lilly."

Billy nodded and put one hand over his mouth, hoping that it would be seen as an expression of grief and not what it really was: an effort to keep himself from cracking up.

"Come on, Billy," said Ralph/Luigi, a trace of an accent in his voice that revealed a childhood somewhere *very* far from Piffling, Indiana. "We don't want to be late."

Luigi Bonaducci threw an arm around Billy and lumbered out of the office, nearly lifting him off the ground in the process. Billy shot a farewell glance at Penny, showing how relieved he was to have such a big, protective cousin helping him through these trying times.

"Okay, let's-a pick up the pace here," said Luigi once they stepped out the front door of Piffling Elementary, his words now rolling out in a thick Sicilian accent. "We got to really break the sound barrier if I'm gonna have you in China by tomorrow morning. Old Maria here is gonna have all her trans-gravitational cylinders working overtime." Luigi pointed at a battered old pickup truck, two wheels on the curb, its body touched up so many times it was anyone's guess as to whether the original color was red or green. "She don't-a look like much, but she's a real spitfire, believe me."

Luigi trotted over and yanked open the passenger door, producing a painful screech. Billy climbed into the pickup and was just about to compliment Luigi on his moxboarer scar when an earsplitting squeal stopped him midsentence.

"Sorry 'bout that," said Luigi, grabbing the blue-furred demi-creatch that Billy had nearly sat on and tossing it into a cardboard box behind the seat. "It's-a not your fault. People sit on Papeesha all the time. She never learns her lesson." Billy watched the strange hamsterlike creature as she licked her fur with an incredibly long yellow-orange tongue. She glared at Billy with her big glassy eyes, silently warning him not to get too comfortable in *her* seat.

Luigi revved the engine and gunned the pickup down the street at a speed that was not entirely appropriate for two guys heading to a funeral. It wasn't long before they had left Piffling Elementary far behind and were whizzing past cows and farmhouses.

"Mr. Vriff-a-nee, he must-a have a lot of faith in you, Billy," said Luigi as he took the truck around a dusty hairpin turn. "Either that," he added with a wink, "or he's-a tryin' to get you killed before you finish your first year of training."

"Tell me about it," said Billy. "It's like he wants me to break the record for most creatch ops in a single month."

"Yeah, well, he's keeping you busy, that's for sure. It's a miracle you still have all-a your arms and legs."

Luigi flicked a few switches that transformed the dashboard from a worn-out strip of cracked plastic to a bank of dials, levers, and flashing lights that would have been perfectly at home in the cockpit of a fighter jet.

Awesome, thought Billy. *Wait'll I'm sixteen and they let me take one of these for a spin.*

"She's not-a got all the latest gadgets like your parents' van," said Luigi as he hung a left and drove the pickup past a chain-link fence and into a vast expanse of farmland, "but she'll get us where we need to go." He paused and added, "Better make sure that seat belt's-a tight, Billy. With this baby, liftoff can be a little rough sometimes."

Within seconds the dirt road they were speeding along became wide enough to serve as an airport landing strip. Billy had taken flight from this road once before, when his parents found it inconvenient to use their usual takeoff spot in Dullard Woods. The vast stretches of farmland on either side of the road provided Luigi with the privacy he needed as his pickup truck took to the skies.

Luigi pulled a lever on the dashboard and up they went into the air. Billy prepared himself for the spectacular view he'd be getting from his half-open passenger window but was treated instead to a mouthful of dust as the pickup slammed back down onto the road. *"Maledizione!"* growled Luigi. Billy felt sure it was not the sort of word Luigi would say in front of his grandmother. "Fly, you old piece of junk!"

The pickup reluctantly did as it was told, this time wobbling precariously from side to side as it slowly gained altitude. A sudden loss of power halted their ascent at thirty feet; then a stomach-whirling dip sent the pickup careening across the surface of a cornfield, shearing cornstalks like a razor shaving stubble.

"Volare! Volare!" shouted Luigi, pounding the dashboard with his fist. "Fly, before we all get-a killed!"

With only seconds remaining before they would plow headlong into a row of towering maples, the pickup lurched up and away, corkscrewing through the air at top speed. Vertigo-inducing views of the cornfield below alternated with blinding blue patches of sky until finally the truck leveled off and followed a more or less steady trajectory high above the Indiana countryside. Billy shot a glance at Papeesha to see if the hazardous takeoff had frightened her. She was sound asleep, evidently unaware that there was any other way for an AFMEC vehicle to operate.

"Sorry about that, Billy," said Luigi. "They keep telling me to get a new truck, but I can't-a do that. We been through so much together." He then grabbed a package from the glove compartment and tossed it into Billy's lap. "Better get started, my friend. You've got a lot of reading ahead of you."

Billy's eyes lit up as he realized what he was holding in his hands: his first ever creatch op prep manual. It was a brown paper package about the size of a small dictionary, with a smudged title stamped on it in dark red lettering:

OPERATION 5738-XJ-12
CHINA, GUIZHOU PROVINCE
HUAQING VILLAGE

"Huaqing," said Billy, struggling with the pronunciation. He knew the word was pronounced "Hwah-ching," but it was tricky getting his mouth to make the right sounds.

A feeling of triumph swept over Billy as he tore open the package and pulled out the contents. Billy had seen AFMEC prep manuals before, but they were always delivered first to his parents, who gave them a thorough going-over before letting Billy have a peek.

There were two slim hardbound books, black with white lettering on the covers:

AFMEC GUIDE TO CHINA

AFMEC GUIDE TO MOUNTAIN CREATCH BIPEDS (ABRIDGED)

They were both timeworn and rough around the edges, their pages yellowed from age and stained with a variety of substances, human blood among them. These books, Billy knew, contained general texts for use on any number of creatch ops.

It was the third book in the package that most interested Billy, the one that had probably been written up and printed out just that morning, containing information specifically related to the current mission. It consisted only of white computer paper, bound by a black plastic spiral strip on the left-hand side. Billy raised it to his nose, inhaling the scent of fresh laser-jet ink. It bore a title that set Billy's heart racing:

OBJECTIVE:

INVESTIGATE INCURSIONS BY RENEGADE ROGMASHERS IN THE VICINITY OF HUAQING VILLAGE

Rogmashers. No way. My first solo creatch op and I might end up head to head with rogmashers? Man, this is going to be incredible.

Billy had read about rogmashers, had even seen grainy footage of them in an AFMEC training class. They were among the largest creatches on earth, and within the category of mountain creatch they were the largest bar none. Many grew to heights exceeding fifty feet, a few reaching sixty feet or more. They were bipeds—a rarity among creatches—and possessed almost unimaginable strength.

"Rogmashers," said Luigi. He whistled and raised his eyebrows knowingly. "No question about it, Billy. Vriff-a-nee is trying to kill you."

CHAPTER 5

The next morning they began to make their descent into Chinese airspace. By this time Billy had managed a brief nap at Luigi's insistence, but not before going over all three books and committing to memory any facts relating to the upcoming creatch op. It looked pretty straightforward: no more than two or three rogmashers were estimated to be involved. They had been making sporadic incursions into human-controlled territory near the remote mountain village of Huaqing. Though there had not yet been any attacks, Billy was being sent to investigate the incursions and assess the threat they posed to the village. If an incursion should occur during Billy's watch, he was fully authorized to use all AFMEC weapons at his disposal to drive the rogmashers back.

Billy had already begun to picture himself doing battle with the rogmashers, and the scenes in his head promised plenty of action. According to the prep manual, he would be equipped with at least three different kinds of weaponry: long-range glaff rifles, paragglian crossbows, and an ample supply of hortch grenades. Billy had some experience with glaff rifles and hortch grenades, but this would be his first time firing a paragglian crossbow in the field. They were hard to control but highly effective if you knew what you were doing. Billy was stoked.

Here's where all that target practice pays off, he thought. *I nailed those simulated pridd lizards in training last month. Hitting a rogmasher should be a piece of cake.*

Cloud cover obstructed the windows of the truck for most of the descent. When "Old Maria" finally broke through, Billy was treated to a spectacular first view of the Chinese countryside.

"Here," said Luigi, handing Billy a pair of powerful AFMEC-issue binoculars. "We're not in Piffling anymore, eh?"

Billy peered through the binoculars. He began studying the landscape for details that might prove useful for the creatch op, but before long he found himself swept up in the sheer beauty of the countryside rolling past below them. There were terraced rice paddies carved into the hills like enormous grassy staircases, straw-hatted men and women knee-deep in water, straightening rice seedlings by hand. Ancient farmhouses dotted the fields, each with carefully tended courtyards and little stone tables where elderly men huddled around pots of tea. Sometimes he'd spot a local temple, its red tiled roof low in the middle and curved up at the edges, as if weighed down by the brightly colored statues of dragons and bearded warriors crowded on top of it.

China, thought Billy. *I can't believe I'm really here.*

"I'll be taking you to the local AFMEC field office," said Luigi. "They'll have all the equipment you need: the rifles, the crossbows, the grenades. But they won't have this." Luigi reached into his shirt pocket and produced a small vial filled with thick yellow-green liquid. Attached to it was a simple silver chain. "Wear it around your neck," he said, handing it to Billy. "You're going to need it, trust me."

"What is it, some kind of anticreatch poison?"

Luigi laughed, long and loud. "No, my friend. It's olive oil. From my grandparents' farm in Sicily. It came from a withered old tree long considered dead. Suddenly one year, this tree, it starts-a bringing forth the biggest, plumpest olives in the whole orchard." Luigi gestured vigorously with his hands. "Now for the people of my village it is a sacred olive tree, a bearer of good fortune. My grandfather, he's no fool. He started putting the oil in vials like this and selling them all around Sicily."

Billy held the tiny bottle up to his nose and sniffed. It was olive oil, all right. "So this is like a rabbit's foot or something."

Luigi drew his eyebrows together in stern disapproval. "It is *no*-thing like a rabbit's foot. It *works,* I tell you."

"What, it protects you?"

"*Yes,* it protects me. I've taken that vial with me on every creach op I've ever been on. And I'm still alive, so it must-a be doing its job." Luigi spoke with the finality of a scientist laying down one of the fundamental laws of physics.

"So now you're giving it to *me?*" asked Billy.

"Yeah, I'm giving it to you. Don't worry, I've got dozens of them back home. I give them to people I care about. My grand-father would have wanted it that way."

Billy didn't really believe in good-luck charms, whether they came from olive trees or the legs of rabbits. But he could see that Luigi took his lucky olive oil very seriously, and that giving it to Billy was a very big deal.

"Thank you, Luigi." Billy put the chain around his neck, allowing the vial to drop beneath his T-shirt. "I'll take good care of it."

"You better believe you will," said Luigi. Then he nodded sagely, adding: "And *it* will-a take good care of *you.*"

Minutes later they descended to an AFMEC airstrip deep

in the Chinese countryside. The pickup's landing was even rougher than its takeoff. The truck slammed into the runway so hard Billy felt sure the axles would crack, and then immediately began skidding across the tarmac at top speed, fishtailing into 360-degree spins as Luigi desperately tried to bring the thing to a stop. When he proved unable to slow it down in time, they shot off the end of the runway and splashed into the middle of a very wet rice paddy.

Never mind the creatches, thought Billy as the truck began sinking into the mud. *You need the lucky olive oil to save you from this pickup.*

Luigi tried for several frustrating minutes to get the truck back up on dry land, then pounded the dashboard with an angry fist, growling more words his grandmother would not approve of.

"Okay," said Luigi. (Billy had never heard the word *okay* sound so thoroughly un-okay.) "I'll take you to the secret entrance on foot, then see if anyone there can tow me out. Stay here, Papeesha," he said to the sound-asleep demi-creatch as he opened the driver-side door. "I'll be right back."

Billy grabbed his prep manuals and followed Luigi, plunging knee-deep into the water of the rice paddy. By the time Billy and Luigi crawled up an embankment to a packed-earth footpath nearby, they were both sopping wet from the thighs down. Billy surveyed the area as he did his best to wring the water from his pants legs.

They were surrounded by steep hills, thick with groves of bamboo that glowed golden yellow in the early morning sun. The air was hot and humid, and smelled faintly of manure. A

lone bird cawed somewhere up in the hills. To one side of the rice paddy stood a crumbling gray farmhouse. Strips of red paper—Chinese characters hand-painted upon them—were peeling away from the top and sides of its doorway, flapping quietly in the warm breeze.

"Does all this belong to AFMEC?" asked Billy.

"Not exactly. The Chinese government leases it to us on a year-to-year basis. They don't allow us to put up fences, though, so we have to keep a low profile in case locals wander through."

Billy smiled as he thought of their landing a few minutes earlier. *Some low profile.*

They followed the footpath out of the rice paddy and up a hill. Soon they were making their way through a Chinese graveyard, weaving between moss-covered gravestones and sculptures of fearsome lions.

"So where's this AFMEC field office?" asked Billy.

"Just on the other side of this graveyard," said Luigi. "Now listen, I should warn you about Chang Ming."

"Chang Ming?"

"He guards the entrance to the field office." Luigi sounded respectful. Or maybe just scared. "He's very tough, and extremely short-tempered. He likes to pick on new guys."

"New guys," said Billy. "Like me."

"Yeah. Don't let him scare you." Luigi paused and added, "Too much. He *will* scare you, it's unavoidable. He scares me, and I've-a known him for years."

Billy swallowed hard. If Luigi was scared of this guy, he must be one dangerous man.

They made their way out of the graveyard and down a path to a small roadside shrine in the shade of an enormous oak tree. The whole thing was no more than four feet square. It consisted of a weathered stone statue on a patch of poured concrete, shielded from the elements by a rickety wooden shelter. Before the statue lay a vase of brittle, dried-out flowers, a sand-filled urn containing burnt stubs of incense sticks, and a plate bearing the shriveled remains of an orange: the offering, Billy imagined, of a poor local farmer.

Luigi cast cautious glances in all directions to make sure they were alone. He then crouched down and placed a hand on the side of the stone sculpture.

K'CHIK

Billy rubbed his chin in admiration as he saw the top of the sculpture swing free on a hinge. Beneath it was an indentation holding a ten-digit keypad, illuminated from within like the buttons of a cell phone. The whole shrine, Billy now understood, had been constructed by AFMEC, expertly camouflaged to blend into the local environment.

Luigi entered a long series of numbers into the pad, then stood at attention. "Be ready," he whispered to Billy. "Chang Ming is coming."

CHAPTER 6

Billy straightened up and waited.

The seconds stretched into a minute.

"He'll be here," said Luigi. "He keeps his own schedule."

Billy had already begun to form a mental picture of Chang Ming. He saw him as Jackie Chan with a catastrophic overdose of steroids. Sort of *Franken*–Jackie Chan.

Another minute rolled by.

Billy's eyes wandered to the base of the shrine. He noticed a mass of cobwebs behind the statue, a leaf from one of the dead flowers caught in it. A sliver of wood, fallen from the roof of the shelter, rolled across the concrete ahead of a light gust of wind. A solitary cockroach skittered out from behind the urn. Billy prepared to squash it with a well-aimed stomp.

"Nooooooooo!" Luigi screamed.

Next thing Billy knew, he was flat on his back, his head buried in weeds, the full weight of Luigi's massive body resting squarely upon him.

"Forgive him, Chang Ming," said Luigi. He rolled off Billy but stayed on all fours. "He's new. He didn't know."

Billy rose on his elbows and glanced in all directions, terrified, expecting the towering figure of Chang Ming to have somehow materialized out of thin air, muscle-bound and ready to pummel him with his bare fists. Only then did he realize that Luigi was talking to the cockroach.

"A new guy, eh?" said the surprisingly deep voice of Chang Ming. He was just over an inch from head to toe. And he was *not* a cockroach, Billy could now plainly see. He was a six-legged creature with some roachlike features but many humanoid characteristics as well. His beady black eyes were protruding from a face that included mandibles and antennae along with teeth, eyebrows, and sideburns.

Billy scrambled into a crouch and turned to Luigi, wondering if this was all some sort of elaborate prank. Chang Ming the Merciless was a little bug dude? But Luigi's terrified face, contorted into an apologetic grimace as he cowered before Chang Ming, told Billy that this was no joke. Chang Ming—little bug dude or not—was to be feared. And a kid who had attempted to squash the guy presumably had more to fear than most.

"What's your name, new guy?" asked Chang Ming. He was standing on his hind legs, two of his remaining legs folded across his tiny chest.

Billy opened his mouth but no words came.

Chang Ming raised one of his last two legs and pointed it at Billy. "What are you, deaf?" He had a slight Cantonese accent, one that would have been right at home in the mouth of a Hong Kong cabdriver. "I asked you a question, buddy. I suggest you answer it."

"B-Billy. My name is Billy. Billy Clikk."

"Click, eh?" Chang Ming cocked his head to one side and spat onto the concrete. The saliva exploded into flame upon hitting the ground, then sent up a surprisingly large cloud of charcoal gray smoke. "Weird name."

Flaming saliva? No wonder Luigi's so scared of this guy.

Luigi pulled a crumpled brown paper bag from his shirt pocket and began opening it with trembling hands. "I brought you some biscotti, Chang Ming. Your favorite: chocolate amaretto."

"Can it, Weeji," said Chang Ming without bothering to look at Luigi. He spat again, this time producing a blast of fire big enough to have come from a flamethrower. The resulting cloud of smoke went straight into Billy's face.

"Now let's get somethin' straight, Billy. You want to live to see your next birthday, you gotta learn one simple rule." He paused and ran a claw across one of his long, curved antennae. "You listenin'?"

"Yes."

"Smart kid. Now repeat after me: *Never.*"

"Never."

"Ever."

"Ever."

"Squash."

"Squash."

"Cockroaches."

"C-cockroaches."

Chang Ming leaned forward and spat so near Billy that the burning ball of saliva nearly hit him. "Think you can remember that?"

"Yes."

"You better hope you do. 'Cause after today if I get word you squashed a cockroach . . . or even *tried* to squash a cockroach . . . or anything that even *looks* like a cockroach . . ." He turned his back on Billy and walked slowly back to the statue. ". . . I'll roast you alive. I'll burn you till your skin gets nice and crispy. Like Peking duck."

Luigi let out a quiet sigh of relief. They were being let off the hook.

As Chang Ming stepped behind the statue, he stopped, spat, and said, "Leave that biscotti on my plate, Weeji."

"Yes, Chang Ming."

"And get rid of that rotten orange, will ya? Hate it when they leave those things." A moment later he was gone.

"Chang Ming is a demi-creatch," said Luigi after Chang Ming was safely out of earshot. "I think you figured that out."

"Yeah, but what . . . I mean, how did he . . . ?"

"Manther roaches," said Luigi as he and Billy rose to their feet. "A kind of ground creatch. Chang Ming used to be a human being like you and me." He paused and reconsidered. "Well, more like *me* than you, sorry. He was six feet tall, two hundred twenty pounds. That was before he and another Affy—a woman by the name of Feng Lei—got bitten by manther roaches during a creatch op."

CHZZZZZ

A humming noise pulsated somewhere underneath the shrine. "Watch it," said Luigi, grabbing Billy by the arm and pulling him a foot or two to one side. "You're in the wrong place."

Billy looked down and saw the ground they were standing on—pebbles, weeds, and all—drop a fraction of an inch. It then broke free from the surrounding earth in a neat circle and began carrying Billy and Luigi underground. As they sank past the rim of earth around them, a disk of pebbles and weeds emerged and slid into place to conceal the hole that had been created.

Whoa. A camouflaged hydraulic sinkhole. Billy's parents had told him about sinkhole "elevators" and how they were used to conceal the entrances to AFMEC field offices, but this was his first time actually riding in one.

"Normally manther venom kills you," said Luigi as they continued their descent, "but get just the right amount and it transforms you into a demi-creatch: half human, half roach. Some victims stay human-sized but have their intellect reduced to the equivalent of a roach's. Others get to keep their human intelligence but wind up the size of a roach. That's how it was for Chang Ming, poor guy. By the time he got back to AFMECopolis his body had absorbed so much venom the transformation was irreversible."

Billy and Luigi descended farther and farther underground. It was cold and very dark, and the smell of motor oil hung in the air. The humming noise grew louder.

"So what happened to Feng Lei?" asked Billy.

"Feng Lei. That's the worst part of the story. The two of them were engaged, you see." Luigi shook his head and sighed. "She was lost in the creatch op and never found. Could have been killed. Probably was. But maybe—just maybe—she's still out there somewhere. That's why Chang Ming is a little touchy about people squashing bugs."

"Oh, man. He's going to hate me forever."

"No, Billy," said Luigi. "You're lucky. He likes you. I can tell."

"You're kidding. How does he treat people he *doesn't* like?"

"You don't want to know," said Luigi. "Let's just say his saliva isn't the only thing inside him that's flammable."

The platform they were standing on carried them down through the ceiling of a brightly lit room. Billy squinted as his eyes adjusted to the light. The room was long and narrow, with a black marble floor, three smooth concrete walls, and a fourth wall built entirely of glass, beyond which lay a wide fluorescent-lit corridor. Three polished steel columns rose from the floor, each vanishing into its own hole in the ceiling: the hydraulic support systems, Billy guessed, for three other camouflaged sinkholes above. They reached the floor of the room, and the humming noise died down, then stopped altogether.

"Welcome to the Guizhou field office," said a girl's voice behind them. "You ready to take on some rogmashers?"

CHAPTER 7

Billy spun around. There, standing with her hands on her hips, was Ana García. She wore a freshly pressed gray AFMEC uniform, a utility belt around her waist, and calf-high mountain-climbing boots. Her long black hair was pulled back into a ponytail, and her caramel-colored skin was even more deeply tanned than usual from a series of recent creatch ops in sub-Saharan Africa.

"Heeey," said Luigi as he strode to Ana's side with several elephantlike stomps and swept her up in a big warm hug. "How's my little bambina? You're getting so tall. No wonder all the creatches are scared of you!"

"Ana!" said Billy as he jumped from the platform to the floor and ran over to her. He wasn't sure whether to hug her or shake her hand—he knew her well, but not *that* well. In the end he did neither: just stood there and gestured awkwardly. "What are you doing here? I thought you were battling sea creatches in Norway."

"That's where I was up until last night. But we had them pretty much under control, you know, so AFMEC high command took me off the job and brought me here. They must have felt my skills were needed on this thing with the rogmashers."

This thing with the rogmashers? Hold on, here. You're coming with me? This is supposed to be my first solo creach op.

"I . . . don't get it. AFMEC is letting you help me out with this?"

Ana laughed. "Good one. Come on, we've got to pick up our equipment and get going."

Good one? What, did I say something funny?

Ana went to a small podiumlike structure in the middle of the floor near the wall of glass. She placed her hand on its upper surface, where an infrared beam hummed quietly as it scanned her palm. Seconds later a small section of the glass wall rose into the ceiling, allowing them all to enter the corridor.

"Sadly I must now bid you both *arrivederci,*" said Luigi with an exaggeratedly formal bow.

"Luigi, I thought I could count on you to help me take out a rogmasher or two," said Ana with a grin.

She's acting like this is her *creach op,* thought Billy.

"Ana, Ana," said Luigi as he took her hand, melodramatically begging for forgiveness. "You know how it pains me to abandon you like this. Never fear, my darling. Billy here will be as splendid an assistant as I could ever be."

Assistant? This just keeps getting worse!

Luigi gave Billy a good strong handshake. "Such a pleasure it was to meet you, Billy. Don't you worry about the rogmashers. You will be safe," he added with a wink, pointing a finger at the vial of olive oil hidden beneath Billy's T-shirt.

Luigi then stepped through a nearby door and went off, presumably in search of someone to help tow his truck out of the rice paddy.

"Come on, Billy," said Ana as she marched down the corridor. "We've got to get you suited up." She ran her eyes over Billy's T-shirt and still-soggy blue jeans. "Don't want the rogmashers to see you looking like this." Ana laughed. Billy didn't.

"Look, Ana," said Billy as he quick-stepped to keep up with her, "there must be some kind of mistake here. This is *my* creach op." He held the prep manuals out for her as evidence. "See?"

Ana's eyes darted back and forth between Billy and the prep manuals. "Billy, that's so cute. You think getting the prep manuals means this is your creach op?"

Cute?

"Well, if it *doesn't* mean that . . . then what does it mean?"

"I've got the very same manuals, Billy. They were given to me last night. You got the prep manuals because your parents can't go with you this time, that's all."

Ana turned a corner and stopped before a door marked CHANGING ROOM. "First stop. I picked out a nice clean suit for you. No bloodstains. It's *so* hard to find AFMEC uniforms like that, you know." Ana nodded in a way that suggested it was time for Billy to thank her.

"I'll be right out," said Billy. He shut the door a little harder than was strictly necessary.

Billy grumbled as he changed into the gray jumpsuit and

laced up the pair of mountain-climbing boots Ana had selected for him. The fact that she had chosen precisely the right size clothes and footwear served only to irritate him. "Little Miss Perfect-All-the-Time. Where does she get off elbowing in on my creatch op?" he whispered angrily. "Just wait. She'll start making all the decisions and treating me like her all-purpose gofer boy."

"Don't worry about your coat and gloves," Ana shouted through the door. "I've put them in our transport. And a nice warm scarf, too!"

Billy threw his jeans, T-shirt, and sneakers into a locker provided in the changing room and stepped back into the hallway.

"Nice," said Ana, regarding Billy as if she had dressed him herself. Which she had, pretty much. "*Very* nice. You're too thin, though, Billy. You need to come down to Guatemala and spend a week with my family and me." She flashed him a smile as she turned and led him down a nearby flight of stairs. "Wait until you get some of Mama's arroz con pollo chapina. *Mm.* She'll fatten you up, no problemo."

Billy was determined not to let Ana change the subject.

"Ana, it's not just the prep manuals," said Billy. "When I got the call on my viddy-fone, Dad told me I'd be going solo this time."

"He said that to you?"

Did he? Sure he did. More or less.

"He used those exact words. *Solo creatch op.*"

"That's funny." The way she said the word it came out like "fawny." "Why would your father lie to you like that?"

Ana opened a door at the bottom of the stairs and ushered Billy into a huge, dimly lit underground warehouse. There stood row upon row of tall iron shelves, each stacked top to bottom with AFMEC weaponry. "I'll get the glaff rifles and the ammo," said Ana, "if you get the paragglian crossbows and the hortch grenades. Deal?" She smiled, signaling that the solo creatch op discussion was now officially over.

"Look, Ana." Billy was trying to stay calm. "We need to make this clear at the outset. Whose creatch op is this? Yours or mine?"

"Billy," Ana said. "This is *our* creatch op. Yours *and* mine. Not yours *or* mine." She locked her dark brown eyes on Billy's and stared him down. "Do you have a problem with that?"

Billy took two steps away from Ana. He wasn't sure how to answer the question. So he didn't.

"Hortch grenades," he said. "How many?"

"As many as you can carry."

CHAPTER 8

"No, no, no," said Ana. "Never put the glaff rifles on the floor of the truck, you'll wreck the sight alignment. And the hortch grenades . . . you pile them up like that, you're going to blow us from here to Bolivia."

They were standing inside a barn behind the farmhouse Billy had seen earlier, loading their weaponry into the back of a very small three-wheeled noodle delivery van. Bright red Chinese characters across the sides of the van proclaimed they were delivering lo mein noodles, not a modest cache of weapons calculated to knock a rogmasher on its heels at a hundred yards.

"Put them like this," Ana said. "Crossbows on the bottom, then the rifles, *then* the hortch grenades, evenly spaced."

Aye, aye, Captain.

Billy did as he was told. He'd decided to choose his battles.

If he didn't, he and Ana would be at each other's throats in no time. That didn't prevent him, of course, from saying rude things to her in the privacy of his own head.

"Did you get that extra case of paragglian bolts I asked for?"

"Ana, you never said anything about an extra case of paragglian bolts."

Ana shrugged. "Well, I'm saying it now. Those bolts are the only things that kill rogmashers, you know. There's a dozen per case, and I've only got one case in the van. You don't want us to be caught shorthanded, do you?"

Billy grumbled as he made his way back to the warehouse through a hydraulic sinkhole in the floor. When he got to the shelf where the paragglian bolts were supposed to be, he found nothing but an empty space and a quarter inch of dust.

Somebody has got to get this place organized.

He ended up finding the bolts in an entirely different aisle, next to a stack of pilot's goggles. The case wasn't even clearly marked. The lettering was scuffed and scratched away, leaving only a PARA and the first half of a G.

I guess that's what happens when you get out into the lesser-used field offices. Everything goes to seed.

He grabbed the heavy case and made his way back to the barn. He put the case in the back of the van and joined Ana in the front seat.

"Chang Ming," Ana said into an intercom on the dashboard once Billy had strapped himself in, *"zou ba!"* She turned to Billy and said, "That means 'let's go' in Chinese."

How do you say "Oooh, I'm so impressed" in Chinese?
CHZZZZzzzzzz

A panel in the roof slid open, sending a dusty beam of sunlight down to the floor.

"Next stop," said Ana, pushing buttons on the dashboard

with one hand and gripping the steering wheel with the other, "Huaqing!"

FFFFFWWOOOOOSSH

In a split second the noodle van rose into the air, tilted back to a vertical position, then shot out through the hole in the roof. Moments later they were hundreds of feet above the earth and heading toward the mountains. Billy was envious of Ana's flying skills in spite of himself.

"It won't take long to get there," said Ana. "I'd go over those manuals one more time if I were you."

Billy opened the *AFMEC Guide to Mountain Creatch Bipeds,* turning to the already dog-eared section on rogmashers. At the head of one page was a detailed illustration showing the size discrepancy between rogmashers and humans. Terrifying wasn't the word. It wasn't terrifying enough. The rogmasher—a two-legged reptile with lizardlike skin, massive biceps, arms long enough to reach the ground (and then some), and a tiny head that was nevertheless breathtakingly hideous—stood fully fifty feet taller than the silhouetted man beside it.

Billy turned his eyes to the columns of text accompanying the illustration. He had them pretty much memorized by now, but it was worth reviewing the facts one more time.

DIET: Exclusively large mammals. Oxen, horses, yaks, deer, and, on occasion, human beings. The adult rogmasher possesses only six teeth—four cuspids below and two enormous incisors above—but makes skillful use of them when dismembering its prey. Rogmashers are remarkably adept at preserving the skeletal integrity of a carcass so as to facilitate the process of spitting out bones.

LANGUAGE COMPREHENSION: Rudimentary. Rogmashers share information with one another using a unique combination of grunts, roars, hisses, and nonverbal communication strategies such as boulder hurling and violent blows of the fist about the head and neck.

MOVEMENT: Rogmashers are slow-moving creatures but are tenacious and nearly unstoppable once they have settled on a course of action. Their legs make up in brute strength what they lack in speed. Their extraordinary arm length allows for movement on all fours in a gorillalike manner, though the musculature and reflexes are reptilian in all other respects.

DEFENSES: The arms of the rogmasher are its only weapons, but formidable weapons they are. The arm muscles are quite literally hard as iron, propelling the fists forward with staggering force, and with predictably devastating results. Pity the man unfortunate enough to be cornered within an arm's length (approximately forty feet) of an enraged rogmasher. His obliteration is all but assured.

WEAKNESSES: The word *weakness* cannot be easily associated with a rogmasher in its prime. Its leathery skin is invulnerable to the vast majority of AFMEC weapons, and its body chemistry provides it with complete immunity to the effects of any and all tranquilizers. Even normally sensitive bodily regions—eyes, nose, and genitalia—are shielded by impenetrable layers of body armor. A patch of shallow skin beneath the chin provides a possible entry point for projectiles, but rogmashers have learned to carefully limit exposure of this area when in the midst of battle.

SUGGESTED CREATCH OP TECHNIQUES: Glaff rifles are perhaps the best way to keep a rogmasher at bay. The pulsating action of the glaffurious oxide disorients rogmashers for up to five seconds per direct hit to the abdomen. Upon recovery, however, the rogmasher's rage may temporarily escalate its strength two- or even threefold, so agents must exercise caution. Hortch grenades are less effective but useful in slowing rogmashers prior to a strategic retreat. Potentially lethal to the rogmasher is a single bolt from a paragglian crossbow delivered squarely under the chin. It is a highly risky strategy, however, in that the proximity required for the proper trajectory puts the agent well within arm's length of the rogmasher. The death of a hapless soul who has failed to hit the mark on the first try will be as swift as it is painful and messy.

"Painful and messy," said Ana, seeing Billy close the manual upon reaching the end of the entry. "A very odd choice of words, don't you think? If you've been killed, surely it doesn't matter if the creatch that's done you in is tidy or not."

"Heck, if I'm going to die I *want* it to be messy," said Billy. "Make those Affys on the cleanup crew work extra hard recovering my remains."

"Billy," said Ana, rolling her eyes, "you have such a strange sense of humor."

"Better—"

—*than no sense of humor at all,* Billy was going to say, but he stopped himself just in time.

"Better what?" asked Ana.

"Better . . ." Billy reopened the manual and fumbled back to the beginning of the entry. "Better read this one more time. In case I missed something."

CHAPTER 9

When Ana brought the van in for a landing on a gravel road high in the mountains of western Guizhou Province, the air temperature was cooler by a good thirty degrees. A late afternoon mist had rolled in, muting the sunlight and turning the pine trees on both sides of the road into pale silhouettes. Billy could see his breath, and he was grudgingly grateful for that "nice warm scarf" Ana had packed for him. It wasn't cold enough to snow, but it was pretty close.

Using a navigational computer screen hidden under the dashboard, Ana was able to guide them through the unmarked mountain roads leading to Huaqing. The prep manuals had provided a few simple facts about this remote village: an estimate of the current population (a mere one hundred forty-six, according to the most recent census), the meager local industries (timber, a bit of farming, and precious little else), and a brief rundown on their AFMEC contact in town, a woman named Lin Mei Jun. (She was from a larger city down in the valley and had been moved into Huaqing soon after the first rogmasher sighting.) But nothing could have prepared Billy and Ana for the spectacular location of Huaqing. As their van turned a corner and the village came into view, the two of them gasped.

Huaqing was built on a quarter-mile-wide strip of land jutting out from an enormous cliff face, which itself jutted out from the pine-covered mountain range surrounding it. The whole village stood in the shadow of the cliff, which loomed over it like a gigantic protective hand. Ramshackle houses were packed so tightly there barely seemed room for footpaths between them, much less roads. The old wooden buildings leaned in toward one another until their tiled roofs nearly touched. It looked as if the next strong gust of wind could send the whole village tumbling into the valley below.

"Why would someone build a village in a place like this?" asked Ana. "It's crazy."

"It's a little nuts, yeah," said Billy. "But I'm guessing Huaqing wasn't always a village. First came the temple. Check it out." He pointed to a red-roofed building at the very edge of the town, perched in the most precarious spot of all, right where the land dropped off at a near ninety-degree angle. "The Chinese love putting temples way up in the mountains like this. I'll bet Huaqing used to be just a temple until they put this road through."

Ana reached over and popped open the glove compartment. "Better switch on my creatch detector," she said. She took out a small electronic device about the size of a CD player and handed it to Billy.

Sweet. Can't wait until they let me have one of these.

Billy had used his parents' creatch detector once or twice before but still didn't have one of his own. Only full-fledged Affys were entrusted with them, since they contained technology that in the wrong hands could be retooled to detect the movement of Affys. Billy pushed a button on the side. A small screen lit up on the top of the device, showing a simple map of their current location. A glowing blue dot in the center stood for Ana, the only full-fledged Affy in the region at the moment. If there were any creatches within a one-mile radius, they would show up as red dots at various points north, south, east, and west of the blue dot. The screen currently displayed no red dots.

"Nope," said Billy. "No rogmashers around right now. They must have seen us coming and taken off."

"Ha ha ha."

"Wow, we're pretty close to the zone," said Billy, pointing at a dotted green line on the left-hand side of the screen. The zone: it was the Affy way of referring to the demarcation line, the official division between human- and creatch-controlled territories as established by the World Creatch Accord of 1816.

"Yes," said Ana. "Huaqing's location is dangerous in more ways than one. Just three miles from the creatches. It's no wonder there have been some sightings."

"Yeah, but there's barely room in this village for a chicken coop, much less the oxen and horses that a rogmasher feeds on. Why would they bother messing around with Huaqing?"

"That, my friend," said Ana, "is what we're here to find out."

They crossed a large wooden bridge with iron guardrails. As they entered Huaqing, it became clear just how small the town really was. The main street—the *only* street—was so narrow you could make a traffic jam with just two cars. Elderly white-haired women with walkers made their way up cobblestone alleyways twisting between the dilapidated houses. Darkly tanned men squatted in gardens tucked into impossibly small spaces, watering rows of cabbage, watercress, and bok choy. A hooded beggar sat on a small wooden stool, feebly drawing a bow back and forth across a battered old musical instrument Billy recognized as an erhu.

In the center of the village was a shadowy outdoor market. Vendors sat behind crates of vegetables and racks of bright red sausages. Billy sniffed hungrily at the potent mix of aromas surrounding a cluster of food stalls they passed: steamed dumplings, fried rice, and a big vat of hot and sour soup.

It didn't take much to attract attention in a town like Huaqing. Even with tinted windows preventing anyone from seeing Ana and Billy, children pointed and stared as they drove by. These kids were intimately familiar with the vehicles that came through the village on a regular basis, and this noodle delivery van definitely wasn't one of them.

"Mei Jun has arranged to meet us at the temple," said Ana. "That's where we'll get briefed on the latest developments."

Ana drove the van down a potholed concrete road leading to the temple, pulled it off onto a narrow strip of grass, and killed the engine. She and Billy both jumped out and walked quickly around to the side of the temple facing the ravine. Even before they had set foot on the temple steps, they were greeted by a small Chinese woman with short black hair and a big bright smile.

"*Huan ying, huan ying,*" she said. "Welcome to Huaqing. I'm Mei Jun, Sino-AFMEC relations. You must be Ana. You must be Billy. Come inside, come inside. You got here so fast! How'd you do it? Transgravitational propulsion, right? Incredible!" Mei Jun was either very proud of her English, or else she always talked a mile a minute regardless of what language she was speaking.

"Please take off your boots," she said as they reached the top of a stone staircase, where a single wooden step allowed them entrance into a small kitchen off to one side of the temple. "Sorry for the trouble. Chinese custom, right? Here. Slippers. Pink for you. Blue for you. Great." She allowed time for a single breath of air, then: "You'll have some tea? I'll put the kettle on. You like *longjing*? Green tea. I bought it last month in Hangzhou. Very nice with melon seeds. You eat melon seeds? I'll let you try some. They're good."

Ana and Billy removed their boots and joined Mei Jun at a Formica table in the middle of the cluttered little kitchen. While Mei Jun busied herself with the tea and talked about everything from the price of melon seeds to the flat tire she'd gotten riding her motorcycle up from Zunyi, Billy took in the details of the room. A framed brush painting of mist-shrouded mountains dominated one wall, while another was given over to a refrigerator and a rusty old stove. Billy marveled at how hand-written Chinese characters made even the most insignificant scrap of paper—a grocery list or a while-you-were-out note—look like a work of art.

"So, Mei Jun," said Ana, interrupting a long story about Uncle Tang, the mah-jongg master, "maybe we need to start talking about rogmashers."

"Right," Mei Jun said, then grew silent for the first time

since Ana and Billy had laid eyes on her. The smile vanished
from her lips, and her face grew pale. She reached into a nearby
drawer, pulled out a map, and unfolded it onto the table.

The map showed Huaqing and its immediate environs. The
village was at the end of a dead-end road. There was a faint dotted line leading away from the temple, which Billy guessed was
a footpath of some sort, but otherwise the only way in or out
was by way of the bridge Ana and Billy had crossed. A line had

been drawn in red pencil indicating the edge of the zone, along with two Xs well within human-controlled territory. Mei Jun nodded slowly before finally speaking again.

"Yeah, they've been crossing the line." She nodded a little more. "Lots of incursions these last few weeks. Many more than usual."

"More than *usual*?" said Billy. "What, this has been going on for a long time?"

"Huaqing is less than three miles from the demarcation line. Creatches stray across the line fairly regularly. Forest creatches, mainly. Little guys. They keep to themselves. Very few incidents." Mei Jun put a reddish brown teapot and three tiny teacups on the table. "But rogmashers? Unusual. *Very* unusual."

"Why's that?" asked Billy.

"There were battles between Affys and a renegade group of rogmashers late in the nineteenth century. Big battles. Very bloody. AFMEC hit the rogmashers hard, and they learned their lesson. Since then rogmashers have been careful never to pass into human-controlled territory." A teakettle on the stove hissed and sputtered as the water inside it started to boil. "Up until last week."

Mei Jun looked from Billy to Ana and back again, her dark eyebrows tensed and pulled low over her eyes. "Last week a farmer, here . . ." She pointed to one of the Xs deep in the woods. ". . . he found footprints in his field. This big." Mei Jun held her hands a good five feet apart. "I saw them with my own eyes. It was a rogmasher, no question."

"Any missing livestock?" asked Ana.

"No. Nothing. Just footprints." Mei Jun frowned at the map. "Like the rogmashers were . . . taunting us. Showing us they can enter human-controlled territory any time they like. Even for no reason."

"Weird," said Billy. "Any direct sightings?"

"Just one. The day before yesterday. Here." Mei Jun pointed at the remaining X before rising to take the kettle off the stove. "Children playing in the woods on the south side of the village. They say they saw a giant gorilla, fifty feet tall. Said it growled at them. Broke a tree in half." Mei Jun poured steaming hot water into the three small cups, warming them thoroughly before dumping the water in the sink and putting tea leaves in the pot. "Brave little children, they didn't even seem scared when they told me about it."

"Leaving footprints on farmland," said Ana. "Breaking trees. What are they up to?"

Mei Jun gave Billy and Ana a worried glance as she placed a cup of freshly poured tea before both of them.

"Something here in Huaqing they're . . . trying to get?" she asked.

Billy studied the map. The two red Xs were less than half a mile from the bridge leading into Huaqing.

"Whatever they're up to, we'll figure it out," said Ana, in a very take-charge voice. She took a sip of tea, then rose from the table. "Come on, Billy. Let's go to that farm and check out those footprints."

CHAPTER 10

"Wow," said Billy. "That farmer must have totally freaked when he saw these."

Billy and Ana were at the farm where the rogmasher footprints had been found. It was late afternoon, but the thick fog rolling in from the valley made it hard to get a sense of where the sunlight was coming from.

"No doubt about it." Ana was taking snapshots with her viddy-fone, which doubled as an AFMEC digital camera. "These were made by a rogmasher."

Seeing the footprints up close, Billy realized Mei Jun had actually underrepresented their size. These things were six and a half feet long. Billy marveled at how deeply the rogmasher's feet had sunk into the gravelly mountain soil, a testament to the staggering weight that rested upon them. Several dozen cabbages, unlucky enough to have fallen underfoot, were now flat as lily pads.

"These footprints were made very carefully," said Billy, down on all fours to make a thorough examination. "Deliberately. You can tell by how well defined they are. Almost like the rogmasher *wanted* someone to find them."

"Not necessarily." Ana took a few more snaps, then put the viddy-fone away. "Rogmashers don't think things through like that. I'll bet you this little guy just wasn't in a hurry."

"*Little* guy?"

"This was a young adult. You can tell by the length of the toes."

Ana was right, Billy knew. But he didn't like her dismissing his theories. She might have been doing this stuff a lot longer than him, but that didn't mean her ideas were automatically better than his.

"The footprints head off in that direction," said Billy, pointing at a forest of pine trees at the edge of the farm. "I say we grab our weapons and follow these tracks."

Ana nodded. "Let's go."

Billy and Ana went to the van and took as much weaponry as they could carry. Ana strapped a glaff rifle to her back and carried a paragglian crossbow in her hands. Billy did just the opposite. They both attached two hortch grenades to their belts. (It was impossible to attach any more. Hortch grenades were the size of pineapples, and even one on each hip was pushing it.)

Billy took a deep breath as he picked up his glaff rifle. He was a little scared, there was no denying it. But he was also psyched.

Maybe we'll run into a rogmasher out there in the woods. Wish I had clocked a few more hours of glaff rifle target practice back at AFMECopolis. Still, you can't beat on-the-job training.

Switching on the creach detector, Billy and Ana began following the tracks. Finding the trail across the farm was a cinch. But once they got into the woods the tracks became harder to detect. For every spot where a clean footprint remained, there was a stretch of rocky, pine-needle-strewn ground that allowed little in the way of footprints, even from a beast that tipped the scales at ten or fifteen tons. But every time they thought they'd lost the trail, the broken branches of trees overhead would serve as a secondary path showing them the way.

For Billy the initial excitement of the rogmasher hunt soon gave way to a deep sense of unease. The terrain grew steadily more craggy and mountainous, and there were plenty of massive rocky outcroppings for one or several rogmashers to hide behind. The fog was getting thicker by the minute, even as the last of the daylight began to seep away. Billy became keenly aware of how far away they were from the farm, from their remaining weaponry, from the village of Huaqing itself.

But there was something else. It was the sense that they were being led into this. As if the rogmashers wanted them to be out here, isolated, hunting around in the woods. Billy had followed creatch trails before. They were generally haphazard and erratic. This trail seemed too deliberate, too straight, too . . . logical.

"Here," Ana said, showing Billy a button on the cuff of her jacket. "Ever use these before?" She pushed the button and fluorescent stripes glowed pale green across her shoulders and along her arms. The jackets they were wearing were an AFMEC innovation: clothing that provided Affys with their own source of light everywhere they went, without having to carry a lantern or a flashlight. The first time Billy used one he feared it would turn him into an obvious target for creatches. Then he remembered that creatches had perfect night vision anyway: they were already obvious targets, and the added light didn't even enter into the equation. Billy clicked the same button on his jacket and they continued on their way, illuminating the woods like a pair of humanoid fireflies.

"Anything on the creatch detector?" Billy asked.

"No, Billy." Ana gave him a look of mild irritation. "And you know what? I don't think it's necessary for you to ask that question every thirty seconds."

"Give me a break, all right, Ana? I just want us to be prepared if anything shows up, that's all."

"Here." Ana handed Billy the creatch detector. "You keep an eye on the thing and stop bugging me about it."

Ooh, excuse me for bugging you, Your Highness.

Soon after Billy began carrying the creatch detector, a tiny orange panel illuminated near its edge.

"Ana," said Billy. "Don't tell me you forgot to put in a fresh power cell."

"Of *course* I put in a fresh power cell. What do you think I am, an Affy-in . . . you know, a beginner?"

Billy gritted his teeth. He was pretty sure that Ana had been about to say "an Affy-in-training" but had managed to stop herself before she said it.

"Yeah, well it couldn't have been *that* fresh," said Billy. "This thing's running out of juice already."

"Impossible." Ana took the creatch detector from Billy and inspected it. "I don't understand this. It can't be. It was a brand-new power cell, I *swear.*"

"How well do these things work when they're running low?"

Ana brushed a stray strand of hair from her forehead. "Not so well. They can give false negative readings." She sighed. "I've got spare power cells back in the van. We'll put in a new battery when we get back."

"Why don't we go back and put one in now?" asked Billy. "There could be a creatch out there and we don't even know it."

"Billy, will you please calm down? Rogmashers make big noises, you know." She stomped her feet, as if needing to explain the concept to a three-year-old. "Boom. Boom. Boom. We'll hear them coming."

"I know that, Ana. I'm not an idiot."

"Good. So let's keep going a little more."

"I *knew* you were going to do this." Billy realized that he'd said more than he wanted to, but it was too late.

"Do what?" Ana put her hands on her hips. "What is it that you *knew* I was going to do?"

Get it out in the open. You might as well.

"I knew you were going to take over my creatch op and then start treating me like your little assistant boy. And you are. You're making all the decisions. You're not even listening to any of my ideas."

"Your creatch op," said Ana. "*Your* creatch op."

"Okay, *our* creatch op. But you're not treating it like that. You're calling all the shots, and I'm supposed to just nod and say 'As you wish.' "

Ana took a deep breath. "Billy. You are an Affy-in-training. I am an Affy. When there is a disagreement over procedure, I win. I'm sorry, but that's the way it is."

Billy said nothing. He turned his face to the ground.

"Look, Billy. I'm here. And I'm not going anywhere." Ana leaned her head down, forcing him to meet her gaze. "So you better just learn to get along with me."

A few silent seconds passed.

"I will listen to your ideas. When they make sense." She turned and continued hiking through the woods. "Now, come on. We'll go a little farther, and if we don't see anything we'll turn back."

They kept going. Billy was angrier than ever but was now determined to keep his mouth clamped shut.

She's, like, the bossiest girl on earth. When we get back to AFMECopolis I'm going to tell them never to send me on a creatch op with her again. Ever.

Several minutes later, in a hollow formed by some mammoth black boulders, they came across the carcass of a deer. It had been reduced to a mere skeleton, the meat neatly removed from its bones. A few flies buzzed about, competing for what little flesh remained. Ana and Billy set their weapons on the ground and crouched down to get a closer look.

"Here's a test for you, Billy. How many days ago was this deer killed?" She was acting as if the little spat they'd just had was already a distant memory. Billy was not so quick to forget, but he knew he had to make an effort to stay on good terms with Ana. They were here to battle creatches, not one another.

"Give or take a day," Ana said.

Billy had done poorly on the section of his Affy exams that related to this very subject, Remains of Creatch Prey: Recovery and Analysis. He was simply more interested in battling a monster than calculating the age of its last lunch. He knew it was something he'd have to work on, though, if he was going to become a well-rounded Affy.

Billy swatted the flies away to get a better look at the

tendons and cartilage. The degree to which it had decayed was one of the key clues to dating a carcass.

"Hard to say," he said, poking at the rib cage with a stick. "A day? Two days?"

"You've got a long way to go, Billy." Ana held up the deer's skull and began talking to it like an old friend. "You poor little guy. He gobbled you up five days ago, didn't he?"

"Here, give me that," Billy said. He held the skull up and adopted a high-pitched voice to create a snarky deer's answer to Ana's question: "No, lady. You've got it all wrong. It was three days ago, and he didn't gobble me. He chewed very carefully before swallowing."

Ana laughed in spite of herself. "Oh really? I hope he brushed his teeth afterward."

· "Well, yes," said Billy, "as a matter of fact he di—"

GYYOOOOOOAAARRRR

A rogmasher. It was right there in front of them.

CHAPTER 11

The rogmasher had been hiding behind the rocks the whole time, waiting. Now it was rising from a crouching position, rising . . . rising . . . over thirty feet tall . . . over forty. When it was finally upright it stood nearly fifty feet tall. Its reptile skin was shiny and wet with condensation. Its massive scaly arms glowed green in the eerie light of the AFMEC jackets. Its horrific face—compact, slimy, twisting in on itself like a Halloween mask turned inside out—was all eyes and teeth and quivering green-gray flesh.

Billy and Ana jumped back and took defensive positions. They had both made the mistake of leaving their weapons more than an arm's length away and now had to waste frantic seconds scrambling to reclaim them.

GYYOOOOOOAAAARRRRR

The rogmasher roared again, throwing its head backward, hurling its guttural howl into the pines. Raising one of its fists into the air, it snorted and brought it down to the earth in a slow, unstoppable arc.

FFWHAAAM

Pine needles and shards of stone shot into the air. The ground shook with the intensity of an earthquake. Taking two or three thunderous stomps forward, the rogmasher bared its teeth for a prolonged growl, sending spittle spattering onto Billy's face and blasting his nose with the stench of half-digested animals.

Ana was the first to get her paragglian crossbow out, raised, and properly aimed. By the time Billy had his glaff rifle out and into position, Ana had taken her first shot.

Fwissssshhh

BOAM!

A purple-blue fireball lit the trees as the rogmasher staggered back from Ana's blow. The pulsating paragglian bolt protruded from the beast's chest about a foot below its collarbone: tantalizingly close to its weak spot, but not close enough.

Now it was Billy's turn.

BRAM

BRAM

BRAM

The shots of the glaff rifle echoed across the mountainside as orange firebolts struck the rogmasher three times in the abdomen. The chamber holding the glaffurious oxide would now require five seconds to reheat, so there was little Billy could do but watch and wait as the rogmasher stumbled back and opened its mouth for the loudest roar yet.

I can't kill it with this rifle. The best I can hope for is to keep it distracted while Ana takes another shot.

Something was wrong. Ana was taking far too long preparing for her second shot.

"Hey, Ana. Any day now, all right?"

"It's my paragglian crossbow," said Ana, keeping an eye on the rogmasher as she struggled to reload. "It's jammed! Just give me another half minute. . . ."

"Half minutes are in *very* short supply right now!"

GYOOOOAAARRR

The rogmasher had now taken hold of a massive boulder some twenty feet away. Billy watched as it lifted the rock into the air, sending a spray of dirt and pine needles tumbling to the ground.

"It's gonna crush us with that thing!" Billy raised his glaff rifle and prepared to fire. The glaffurious oxide chamber had not yet reheated, but it would only be another second now, two at the most.

The rogmasher took two huge stomps toward Ana and Billy . . .

DROOM

DROOM

. . . then lifted the boulder all the way above its head.

"Aim for the elbows!" said Ana.

"The *elbows*? But—"

"Just do it!"

GYYYOOOOOOAAARR

The rogmasher sent one more roar echoing through the trees as it prepared to drop the Dumpster-sized boulder—easily big enough to crush several people at once—right on top of its cornered foes.

Billy gritted his teeth and . . .

BRAM

BRAM

. . . fired shots into both of the rogmasher's elbows in rapid succession. He watched in amazement as the rogmasher's arms shot out involuntarily, sending the boulder crashing into the upper reaches of a nearby pine tree.

The rogmasher howled in dismay.

"Great shots, Billy," said Ana as she finally crammed a fresh paragglian bolt into her crossbow. "Now let's see if I can hold up my end of the bargain." Ana aimed and fired.

Fwissssshhhhh

BOOOOOOAM!

Had Ana managed a direct hit on the underside of the rogmasher's chin? It certainly looked that way. Blue sparks shot out from the creature's neck as it dropped to its knees and let out a bloodcurdling screech. But when it rose to its feet again, the second paragglian bolt was lodged just inches away from the base of the neck: painful but not lethal.

Still, the rogmasher had had enough. It bared its teeth at Ana and Billy for one last angry (and extremely foul-smelling) growl, then limped off into the fog, moaning all the way.

Moments later they were alone again, with nothing around them but fog, pine trees, and the silence of an empty forest.

"You okay?" asked Ana. A stone shard had struck Billy on the cheek, leaving a long, bleeding scratch.

"I'll be all right. What about you?"

"I'm fine." Ana peered into the fog where the rogmasher had just vanished. "A little spooked, but fine."

"Thanks for that tip about firing into the elbows."

"It's a trick I heard about from my mother. Never tried it myself, actually."

"Oh, great. Now I owe both you *and* your mother."

Ana grinned. "You better believe you do. I'll have to come up with a nice long list of ways for you to make it up to us."

Billy looked off in the direction the rogmasher had headed. "Do you think it's gone for good?"

"That bolt should keep it out of action for a good day or two." Ana turned to Billy. "It really took us by surprise, didn't it?"

"Yeah." Billy rose to his feet. "Too much of a surprise if you ask me. This whole thing feels like a trap. Think about it. The trail: way too direct, way too easy to follow. The deer carcass left in a spot where we had no easy escape route. It's a lot more sophisticated than a rogmasher could manage on its own."

"Billy, you're getting paranoid. Mountain creatches move in

straight lines all the time. It's nothing unusual. And finding a protected spot to feed is common behavior among all creatches, you know that."

"But it was waiting for us, Ana. *Hiding.* Rogmashers don't hunt like that."

Ana shrugged. "Who says it was hiding? It may have been resting there when we happened to come along."

"Oh, come on, Ana. You think this was all a coincidence?"

"And you think it was all . . . what, part of some big conspiracy?"

Billy took a deep breath and let it out slowly.

"I don't know, Ana. It's just a hunch, but something tells me we're up against more than rogmashers here."

Ana nodded. Billy could see she was trying to be sympathetic, though she didn't agree with his take on things. "So what do you want me to do? Call in reinforcements?"

Billy thought for a moment, then shook his head. "No. Can't take other Affys off their jobs based on a hunch."

"It's getting late," said Ana. "Let's get back to Huaqing. With that rogmasher out there, we can't afford to leave the village unguarded for even a minute."

CHAPTER 12

On the way back to the village Ana tried to put a call through to AFMEC to report on their progress but found the signal blocked. "The mountains," she explained. "They can really cause trouble with communications sometimes. I'll try again tomorrow."

By the time they got back to Huaqing, bandaged Billy's wound, and got something to eat, it was nearly midnight. They agreed to park the van at the bridge leading into town and keep watch during the night, splitting the time into three-hour shifts. Ana went first. At three in the morning she woke Billy up and they switched places.

It was a long, unpleasant three hours: windy and cold. Billy was already itching for another rogmasher encounter, but the only beast to cross his path was nothing more frightening than a scrawny stray dog with a nasty skin problem. So Billy spent most of the night firing imaginary blasts of glaffurious oxide at imaginary creatches, all the while racking his brain for new theories about what the rogmashers were up to.

I'll have to talk to those kids who saw that rogmasher the other day. They ought to be able to provide some clues.

When the sun broke over the eastern mountains around six, Billy was only too happy to switch places with Ana and get a couple more hours' sleep. But after only thirty minutes he was being shaken awake again, this time by Mei Jun.

"Come on, Billy," she said, looking thoroughly refreshed from a good night's rest. "We need to get you some *dou jiang*. Let's go."

"Mmm," said Ana, who was already enjoying a bowl of the soy milk. "This is good. Go get some, Billy. And take some time off while you're at it. We'll go in six-hour shifts until nightfall."

Billy forced himself up and out of the back of the van.

Six hours. Great. I should be able to dig up a lot of info in six hours.

Mei Jun led Billy through a narrow alleyway to the marketplace in the center of the village. "What happened last night?" she asked. "I hear you saw some action."

"Yeah," said Billy, "we had a little run-in with a rogmasher.

Sent it packing without too much trouble, though." Billy was trying to sound casual, but his voice wasn't very convincing.

"Really?" Mei Jun turned to him with raised eyebrows. "Looks like trouble to me." She pointed at the cut on his cheek.

Billy chuckled nervously and found himself with nothing smooth to say in response.

Mei Jun led Billy to a couple of rusty steel stools next to a wooden table in the middle of the marketplace. They were surrounded by villagers, most of them wrinkled old men mumbling gruffly to one another in Mandarin. *"Dou jiang,"* Mei Jun called out to a heavyset woman stirring steaming soy milk in a giant black wok. *"Liang ge."*

"Look, Mei Jun," Billy said after the woman brought two bowls of the yellow-white liquid and plunked them down on the table, "I need your help."

"You got it," said Mei Jun before taking a big slurp of *dou jiang.* "What do you need?"

"You know how you said some kids saw a rogmasher out in the woods south of the village?"

"Two days ago, yeah. What about it?"

"I need to talk to those kids." He blew on his soy milk to cool it down. "I want to ask them some questions."

"And you need me to translate," said Mei Jun, nodding. "No problem. I can set that up for later this morning. So what's going on?" She leaned forward. "You figure out what these rog-mashers are up to?"

"No." Billy took a sip of the soy milk. It was piping hot and very sweet, a bit like melted ice cream that had been warmed on a stove. "But with a little more information I could at least come up with some theories."

"You leave it to me," said Mei Jun. "I'll help you with the interviews." She raised a finger. "I can help you with the theories, too."

"Yeah?"

"You bet I can. I've seen a lot of creatch ops come and go. I've seen Affys fight amphibious chran-g'tanns on the Yangtze River. I've seen Affys up to their ears in purple goo in the sewers underneath Shanghai. I've seen . . ." Mei Jun paused for another gulp from her bowl. ". . . I've seen a lot."

"Sounds like you have," said Billy. "Ever consider becoming an Affy?"

Mei Jun frowned and shook her head.

"Why not?"

"Too much slime," said Mei Jun before slurping the last of her *dou jiang.* "Come on," she added, motioning for Billy to drink faster. "I want to go see those kids. You've got me curious now."

Within an hour Mei Jun had arranged a meeting between Billy and three of the children who had seen the rogmasher. They sat together, two boys and a girl, on a heavy stone bench outside the local elementary school, a crumbling concrete building that looked like it hadn't had a fresh coat of paint since the days of Mao Tse-tung. They each wore simple navy blue and white uniforms. The boys had near identical bowl haircuts and the girl had her hair woven into two long braids. They were strangely motionless for seven-year-olds.

Billy began by asking them about the rogmasher. "Was it very tall?"

"Hen gao ma?" was Mei Jun's translation.

None of the children answered right away. The schoolyard was quiet, apart from the whines of a nearby stray dog.

Then all at once the girl spoke: *"Hen gao,"* she said, which Mei Jun translated as "very tall." *"Hen gao, hen gao,"* said the two boys. Billy couldn't help thinking they were agreeing because of some prearranged pact rather than out of shared experience.

Weird. It's as if seeing a rogmasher wasn't such a big deal to these kids.

"Were you frightened? Was the monster scary?"

Mei Jun translated the questions. There was another long pause. The stray dog barked at something.

Again, the girl answered first. *"Hen kong bu,"* which Mei Jun translated as "very scary." *"Hen kong bu,"* said the boys, repeating the words like trained parrots.

Scary? Could have fooled me. Something's up with these kids. Did someone prep them for this interview?

Billy remembered something he'd been told during his training at AFMECopolis. One of his teachers, Dr. Kasparov, was coaching him on investigative techniques. *"Here's something to try, Billy,"* he'd said, *"when you sense that a witness is giving you incomplete information—memorized answers rather than spontaneous responses. Try throwing in an entirely random request, something they couldn't possibly have anticipated. Ask them what their favorite flavor of breakfast cereal is. Make them crow like a rooster. If it embarrasses them, so much the better. They will reveal something of what they are trying to hide. They always do."*

"Tell them to sing me a song," said Billy, trying his best to

make it sound like this was the next logical step when interviewing kids who'd seen a creatch.

Mei Jun gave Billy a confused look. "A song?"

"Yeah, a song."

"What kind of song?"

"A children's song. Pick one that's really popular in China."

Mei Jun shrugged and asked them to sing *"Liang Zhi Lao Hu,"* which she translated as "The Two Tigers."

This time there was an even longer pause. The children's mouths hung open. Not in embarrassment, but in simple ignorance. They clearly didn't know the song.

"Ni bu zhidao ma?" asked Mei Jun. Billy didn't need a translation to know that this was something along the lines of "Don't you know it?" Mei Jun began to hum the tune for them, but Billy immediately motioned for her to stop.

"No. Don't sing it for them. Let them sing it on their own."

Mei Jun frowned, then sat back and folded her arms, a have-it-your-way look in her eyes.

The children looked increasingly nervous. Billy had known that the question would throw them off balance a bit, but he certainly hadn't foreseen this dumbstruck response.

They don't know the song. They've never even heard it before.

"What's the problem?" asked Billy. "It's a popular song, right?"

"Yes," said Mei Jun. "I'm sure they know it. Every Chinese child knows *'Liang Zhi Lao Hu.'*"

"All right, so let's hear it."

Mei Jun told them once more to sing the song. The children were at a total loss, as if they'd been asked to recite the Gettysburg Address.

The stray dog moaned and chased its tail.

"I don't like this," said Billy. "These kids are acting really stra—"

Suddenly, all at once, all three of the children began to sing *"Liang Zhi Lao Hu."* They sang it in perfect unison, each hitting the notes at precisely the same moment. The song that they hadn't known at all seconds earlier now came across as something they had been rehearsing for just such an occasion.

They know it now, but they didn't know it a second ago?

Mei Jun smiled at Billy. "I told you they knew it. They're good Chinese kids. Of course they know it."

Billy drew his eyebrows together and rubbed his jaw.

Something's not adding up here. These kids are hiding something from me, and it goes way beyond what they saw out there in the woods.

"You okay, Billy?" Mei Jun put a hand on his shoulder. "I think maybe you need some rest."

Rest? No way. What I need is more clues. And more time to think.

"Yeah," said Billy. "I could use a little break."

CHAPTER 13

Billy thanked Mei Jun for her help with the interview, then excused himself, leaving her with the impression that he would take her advice and head back to the van for some rest. Instead, he wandered through the narrow streets and alleyways of Huaqing, trying to come up with an explanation for the children's unusual behavior.

They were coached for that interview. Someone told them what to say and what not to say. Who would go to the trouble of interfering with Affy interviews?

Billy climbed a flight of concrete steps between two weathered wooden buildings, turned a tight corner, and passed a row of potted plants.

Why would anyone in Huaqing want to do that? Then again,

it could be someone . . . not from Huaqing. Someone who doesn't want AFMEC to find out what's really going on here.

Billy considered the possibility of a plot against AFMEC. He'd studied a number of such cases in two of his favorite classes: Introduction to Creatch Sympathizers, and Anti-AFMEC Tacticians and Their Preferred Methods. Those who worked on behalf of creatches were known to pressure Affy interviewees into withholding information, and when they did, it generally meant some fairly serious anti-Affy maneuvers were under way.

It would have to be someone Chinese, or at least someone who speaks Chinese. If they're on the list of identified AFMEC enemies, that narrows the field. There's, what, three Chinese speakers on that list that I know of: Tengzhao Han, Kyang Min Ruzzbak, and Ilga Vobbling.

Han was an unscrupulous Chinese mobster who had joined up with the creatch sympathizers for his own personal enrichment. Ruzzbak was a Central Asian nomad who took up the creatch supremacist cause when Affys fatally wounded his grandfather in the remote Chinese province of Xinjiang. Vobbling was a native of Germany but had adopted China as her homeland at an early age. Her anti-AFMEC motivations were born of a twisted, anarchic desire to see creatches rule the earth: she attacked Affys as if it were a sort of blood sport. All three were still at large, and all three were known to have organized creatches in a variety of ill-conceived plots within the borders of China.

Not Han. Not his style. He wouldn't waste his time in a remote village like this. He's strictly a big-city operator.

Ruzzbak? A possibility. It's hard to picture him coaching those kids—easier to picture him locking them up—but he could do it if it meant somehow giving the rogmashers an advantage.

Vobbling? Could be. She's worked with mountain creatches before. Would she go to the trouble of coaching prospective interviewees? Seems like she'd have cut to the chase with an all-out attack by now.

Billy stepped to one side of the alleyway to allow an old man to pass with a rusty blue bicycle. Through a small window at eye level he saw an empty birdcage swaying on a chain.

Let's not forget about Jarrid Glurrik, though. He was a language whiz: Chinese, Russian, Portuguese, you name it. And if I'm right that he's still alive—a big if, for sure—coaching interviewees would be right up his alley. He was a cloak-and-dagger guy, big-time.

As he climbed another flight of lopsided stairs, something caught his eye. It was a simple quarter-inch-thick black cable, snaking its way up a gutter on the side of a battered old building a few doors down from the marketplace. Billy had seen this sort of cable before: it was the type of thing you could buy in an electronics store for hooking up your stereo system. He tried to follow the lower end of it, but it disappeared into a neatly drilled hole in the wall beside a padlocked door. The other end of it ran up to the top of the roof and out of view.

What the heck is a cable like this doing in a backwater Chinese village? This looks brand-new. Like it was put here just yesterday.

Billy looked up to the roof.

If I could get up there and see what it's attached to . . .

Just then an old man came down the alleyway with a cartload of vegetables. He was coughing and moving at the leisurely pace of someone who didn't much care whether he reached his destination. Eventually he passed, leaving Billy alone in the alley.

Billy glanced over his shoulder and then stacked a few nearby crates one upon the other. He hoisted himself onto the roof. The cable went clear across to the other side of the building. Billy looked around to make sure no one was watching from any of the several windows within sight of him, then climbed across the roof tiles on all fours. A chill wind blew across his back. The dark gray tiles were cool to the touch and somewhat brittle with age. Billy had to move quickly but carefully to avoid damaging anything as he followed the cable's path.

Billy knew he was taking a pretty big chance. If he was going to go by the book, he'd have to ask permission from the village leaders before doing this sort of stuff. Still, if Ruzzbak or Vobbling was pulling the strings behind the scenes, it was going to be permission denied, no question.

Sometimes you have to break the rules.

When he reached the crest of the roof he saw the wire twist off to the right—across a narrow gap between two rooftops—and continue in a straight line to the top of a concrete warehouse in the center of the village. Billy again checked for unwanted witnesses, then quietly made his way from one rooftop to the other, hopping quickly over the shadowy alleyway below.

At this point the climb became more hazardous. The roof tiles were loose and crumbly, and any misstep would result in a very noisy and destructive tumble straight down to the street. Billy swallowed hard and kept moving, making his ascent one gingerly footstep at a time.

He was now high enough to get a good view of most of the village. Rooftops receded on all sides, brown and gray against the pale blue mountains beyond. Nearby telephone lines served as perches for several rows of pigeons, some of whom cocked their heads at Billy for a moment before turning their attention back to the late morning sky.

The cable led Billy higher and higher, until finally he came to the side of the warehouse, at four stories the tallest building in the village. The cable went straight up the two stories that stood between Billy and the top of the warehouse, then disappeared over the edge of the roof. Billy checked for onlookers.

He was now on a patch of roof overlooking the village marketplace. He could even see the table where he and Mei Jun had eaten breakfast that morning. Fortunately there was a drainpipe leading up to the top of the warehouse, and it was just far enough to one side for Billy to scale it without being seen by anyone below. Doing his best not to make a sound, he gripped the drainpipe and started climbing.

The rusty fixtures holding the drainpipe to the wall creaked and groaned as Billy made his way up, foot by foot. When he reached the edge of the roof and pulled himself over it, a gust of wind blasted him in the face and threw dust in his eyes. It took a full minute of furious blinking and eye rubbing to regain his vision, but when he did he was rewarded with a clear path to his goal: the cable weaved across the concrete surface and finally came to an end at the top of a ten-foot-tall aluminum tower. The tower was capped by a toaster-sized black box with miniature megaphone-shaped speakers protruding from it on four sides.

Billy crossed to the tower and climbed up to get a closer look. The box's surface was a smooth semigloss material unlike

anything Billy had seen before. It had no markings of any kind: no manufacturer's logo, no MADE IN CHINA, not even a serial number. The speakers were just over three inches in diameter. The entire apparatus, tower included, was utterly free of any sign of weathering. It looked to have been installed within the past several days.

This thing is superhigh-tech, whatever it is. It looks like it was put here by extraterrestrials.

Billy carefully stepped from one side of the tower to the other and examined the device's upper and lower surfaces, to be sure he wasn't missing anything. There was little left to see, though: no bolts, no seams, no sign of how it had been put together. Billy placed one hand on top of the box. It was slightly warm, with a barely detectable vibration emanating from within. He put his ear against each of the speakers. He heard a hum, low and steady, like a brand-new computer.

What is it? Some kind of PA system? The speakers are so small. They don't look like they'd pump out enough volume to be heard past the edge of the roof, much less down at street level.

Billy checked his watch: 11:45. Time to get back to the van and trade shifts with Ana. He pulled out his viddy-fone and took a dozen or so photos: the box, the speakers, the tower, and its relation to the rooftop. He then jotted down some quick details in a pocket-sized notebook about the dimensions of the entire structure.

Okay. That's all I can do for now. I'll show this stuff to Ana and see if the two of us can't figure out what this thing's used for.

And who's using it.

Billy returned to the edge of the roof and made his way onto the drainpipe. His mind was already racing, trying to connect the speaker-box thing to the various anti-Affy suspects he'd come up with so far.

That thing was state-of-the-art. We can take Ruzzbak off the list, then. He doesn't have the know-how to deal with hardware like that. So there's only two possibilities: Vobbling and Glur—

GRRRAAAAAK!

All at once the drainpipe broke away from the side of the warehouse.

CHAPTER 14

The drainpipe teetered briefly, then dropped like a falling tree. Billy leaped off, trying to land on all fours, but it was too late. He caught a sickening glimpse of a rooftop rushing up to meet him, then . . .

FFWHAM!

chak chak chak chak

. . . chipped pieces of tile shot into the air as he smashed, shoulders first, onto the surface of the roof, then rolled sideways straight down toward the marketplace.

With only a second to spare, Billy maneuvered himself onto his back, jammed both feet into the gutter at the roof's edge, and halted his slide. Dust and tile chips rained down all around him, tumbling past and whirling off into the marketplace. Billy pictured the puzzled faces of the villagers below, craning their necks, asking one another, "What the heck was that?" in Chinese.

For a moment he just lay there, inhaling, exhaling, his heart pounding like crazy. He shielded his eyes and checked all the windows within sight of his current position. From what he could see, he had miraculously managed not to attract any onlookers. At least, not yet.

A minute passed. When no faces appeared at any of the windows, Billy quietly rolled onto his stomach and crawled, inch by inch, back up the roof. He soon found a four-foot concave circle of smashed tiles where he'd first landed. Thankful that he

had not gone straight through into some grandma's bedroom below, he turned his attention to the drainpipe. It was now nearly horizontal. The lower end was still attached to the warehouse, but the rest of it jutted out at a severe angle, displaying several fresh dents and scratches.

Can't leave it like this.

Billy propped the drainpipe back up, straining and suppressing a grunt as he struggled under its weight. Finally it reached the tipping point and he was able to move it back to its original position on the warehouse wall. It had been attached to the wall in three places. The two higher fixtures were beyond Billy's reach, but he was able to jam the rusty bolts of the lower fixture back into the concrete. It was a pathetic stopgap measure—the next rainstorm would probably bring the whole thing right back down again—but it was the best Billy could do at the moment.

He checked his watch: 12:03.

Time's up.

The trip back across the rooftops was mercifully uneventful. Billy breathed a sigh of relief as he stepped onto the crates and climbed back down to street level.

Talk about luck. If anyone had seen that, it would've gone straight into Ana's evaluation report at the end of the creatch op. I've gotta be more careful.

Billy went to the van and joined Ana for a light lunch of *niu rou mian*: beef noodles. Billy told Ana about the PA system and showed her the photos he'd taken with his viddy-fone.

"It *is* pretty high-tech-looking for a place like this," said Ana. "Any theories?"

"I don't know what that thing is for, Ana," said Billy, "but I'm pretty sure it wasn't put there by anyone from Huaqing. I think this village has been infiltrated."

"Infiltrated?"

"Someone's getting to these villagers before we do and coaching them on how to respond to our questions. The kids this morning were acting really weird. Nothing they said was spontaneous. It was like they were reciting memorized answers fed to them by someone else."

"Hm," said Ana, apparently unwilling to agree or disagree with Billy's take on things. "I'll keep that in mind during my interview this afternoon. Mei Jun and I are going to go talk to that farmer who found the footprint."

"Be careful, Ana. I think we're up against more than just rogmashers here."

"Okay, Billy," said Ana after she finished her noodles and rose to leave. "See you at six."

It was a long, quiet afternoon. The creatch detector remained utterly blipless and Billy was left with nothing to do but try to piece together what little information he had so far. Mei Jun stopped by late in the afternoon and they exchanged ideas about who they'd interview that evening during Ana's watch.

"Here's my advice," said Mei Jun. "Go straight to the village leader: Mr. Hu."

"Really?"

"Absolutely. In Chinese society the people at the top always have the best information. If there's anyone in this village who knows what's really going on, it's Mr. Hu."

"Think you can set up an interview with him for tonight?"

"Leave it to me, Billy."

At eight o'clock Mei Jun led Billy through the shadowy streets of Huaqing toward Mr. Hu's home. Night had fallen, and many villagers had lit the red paper lanterns hanging above their front doors. A heavy mist had rolled into the village, muting the already dim light of the streetlamps and making it impossible to see what lurked down darkened alleyways.

When they reached Mr. Hu's door, Mei Jun rang the buzzer.

"You'll like Mr. Hu," she said. "He's a nice guy. Very generous. See this?" She pointed to a jade brooch on her lapel. It had been cut and polished into the shape of hyacinth, and a life-sized one at that. "He gave it to me when I first came to the village."

There was a sound of shuffling footsteps; then Mr. Hu threw the door open and spoke the usual Chinese words of welcome: *"Huan ying, huan ying!"* He looked to be well over sixty years old. He had closely cropped white hair, thick glasses, and a big black mole on one side of his chin. His movements were smooth and agile, like those of a man half his age.

He ushered Mei Jun and Billy into a dark hallway, where they removed their shoes and put on slippers. He then invited them to have a seat in his study, a room lined with books and framed examples of Chinese calligraphy. Against one wall was a large marble table with paper, ink, and a rack of timeworn bamboo brushes.

"Mr. Hu is a real calligraphy master," said Mei Jun while Mr. Hu excused himself to put a kettle of water on the stove. "Look here," she said as she pointed to one of the intricate red squares at the bottom of a nearby scroll. Billy recognized it as the impression left by a chop, a Chinese name stamp. "That's his name: Hu Baiyong."

Billy examined the delicate strokes of black ink that danced across the scroll in lively columns. He knew from his own clumsy attempts at writing Chinese characters that people only reached this level of skill after decades of practice.

Man. This guy is good.

Mr. Hu returned, joining Billy and Mei Jun around a lacquered black table. He and Mei Jun exchanged a few sentences in Chinese. Billy recognized the word *guai wu*—monster—from a Chinese video game he'd played once. Otherwise, he had no idea what they were saying to one another.

Mei Jun turned to Billy and translated. "First of all, Mr. Hu wants to thank you for coming to Huaqing."

Billy smiled at Mr. Hu and gave him his best no-need-to-thank-me-it's-my-job nod. At the same time he noted Mr. Hu's oddly expressionless face. He didn't look particularly glad to have Billy around.

"Mr. Hu also wants you to know," continued Mei Jun, "that as village leader he feels responsible for the lives of everyone in Huaqing. He has been here since the days of the Great Leap Forward. He knows everyone in the village. Has seen their children grow up. Their grandchildren grow up. He promises you he will do everything he can to help you protect Huaqing from anything that threatens it."

Mr. Hu was smiling now, but his eyes were at odds with his mouth. They were glassy, unblinking.

"Great," said Billy, opening his notebook. "Well, first I need to hear about any previous creatch sightings near Huaqing. Even ones from decades ago."

Mei Jun translated. There was a long pause. Then Mr. Hu answered at length. Billy had the momentary sensation of having heard Mr. Hu's voice before, and very recently at that. He searched his brain for an explanation. It was impossible, any way you looked at it. He'd never met the man before in his life.

Mei Jun translated Mr. Hu's answer. Billy uncapped his ballpoint pen and jotted everything down in his notebook, along with his own theories about which creatches—if any—had been seen: *1962: trees uprooted north of the village. Seven-toed footprints nearby. Possibly forest creatches: pugvuggins or long-necked nimribs.*

1971: small furry beings sighted in the woods south of the village. Glowing orange eyes. Roaming snuds?

Even as Billy took notes, he sensed that little valuable information was to be found in anything Mr. Hu was saying. The real story was Mr. Hu himself.

It's like the kids this morning. All these answers sound coached.

Billy proceeded to his next question. "Are there any stocks of food in the village that might lure a hungry creatch?"

Mei Jun translated. Again, a pause. Then came the answer, much shorter this time.

"No. Nothing. Farmer Lin has some pigs. After that, families keep a few chickens here and there throughout the village. Nothing else."

Billy peered into Mr. Hu's eyes. There was a blankness behind them. Billy felt as if he were staring into the eyes of a frog. *All right. Time for another curveball. Gotta throw this guy off balance if I'm going to get anything useful out of him.*

"Very nice calligraphy," said Billy, pointing at one of the scrolls. "You did all these yourself?" Mei Jun raised an eyebrow at this sudden change in the course of the interview but translated Billy's words without comment.

Again, a pause. This time longer than before. Finally Mr. Hu nodded and said, *"Dui, dui. Dou shi wo xie de,"* which Mei Jun translated as "Yes, yes. I did them all."

Billy rose and crossed the room, coming to a stop next to the marble table. "I've never had the chance to see a calligraphy master at work. Could you give us a little demonstration?"

Mei Jun cleared her throat and turned to Billy with a frown. Billy gave her a reassuring look and motioned for the translation. Mei Jun obliged.

There was another long pause; then Mr. Hu's eyes betrayed a look of mild panic. Before he could say anything, a whistling sound pierced the air. Mr. Hu rose with an expression of great relief. *"Pao cha, pao cha,"* he said as he trotted off to the kitchen to take the boiling water off the stove.

"Billy," Mei Jun said, "what does a calligraphy demonstration have to do with creatches? We don't want to waste Mr. Hu's time."

"Trust me, Mei Jun. This is part of the interview process."

Mei Jun frowned again. "Okay. But don't get carried away with this kind of stuff. In China it's very important to show respect to elders."

"I'll be careful."

She's right, thought Billy. *But I'm on to something here, I know it.*

The fragrance of Chinese tea filled the room as Mr. Hu returned from the kitchen. He was carrying a dark brown teapot and three matching cups, which he proceeded to set on the table. Billy returned to his seat.

Mr. Hu spoke at length with Mei Jun in Chinese, which she periodically translated. He was singing the praises of the tea they were about to enjoy, and Mei Jun was a very receptive audience.

"Silver Needles tea," she told Billy with a knowing look. "Very hard to find. Not cheap, either."

Billy smiled and thanked Mr. Hu as he raised one of the tiny brown cups to his lips. The tea was bitter, but tinged with sweetness and a lingering floral aftertaste. "Delicious," Billy said, producing a satisfied smile from Mei Jun.

There was a silent moment of peaceful tea appreciation, which Billy effectively destroyed with his next sentence: "Now how about that calligraphy demonstration?"

Mei Jun groaned.

Billy was undeterred. "Mr. Hu, I'm sure you wouldn't mind writing a character or two for me."

Mei Jun sighed and translated Billy's request.

Mr. Hu looked thoroughly unsettled. It was as if he'd been asked to do a handstand or juggle power saws. He stuttered a bit, then mumbled a few quiet syllables. Mei Jun said, "He says he's not as good as he used to be."

Billy waved Mr. Hu's modesty aside. "Come on. Just write one word for me. How about *fearless*? *Wu wei.* It's just two characters, right?" Billy knew exactly what the characters for *wu wei* looked like. They were sewn onto the back of his favorite jacket back in Piffling, the one he wore for skateboarding competitions.

Mr. Hu made no sign of rising from his chair. He looked trapped.

This guy's not the real deal. If he were, he'd have no trouble showing off his calligraphy.

"Let's make this as easy as possible," said Billy. He turned to a fresh sheet of paper, rotated the notebook until it faced Mr. Hu, then slid it across the table along with the ballpoint pen. *"Wu wei."* He smiled a hard smile at Mr. Hu. "Can't be that difficult."

For a moment Mr. Hu looked truly frightened.

He's a fake. His handwriting is probably no better than Mei Jun's.

"Come on," said Billy, sensing that he had Mr. Hu cornered and vulnerable. "Either write the words, or tell us the real reason why you don't want to."

All he needs is a little prodding. If I can make him believe that I already know what he's up to, he'll snap and reveal everything.

Billy turned to Mei Jun, who—fearful of offending Mr. Hu—had stopped translating. "Tell him I know what's going on here in Huaqing. Tell him I know he's a part of it."

"Billy . . ."

"Please, Mei Jun. You've gotta trust me on this. It's going to pay off, big-time."

Mei Jun swallowed hard. "Okay. I'll tell him you know what's going on in Huaqing, but I'm not going to accuse him of doing anything wrong."

"All right, all right," said Billy. "Just tell him . . ." He paused and chose his words carefully, lowering his voice to a near whisper. "Tell him if he's got anything to get off his chest . . . now's the time to do it."

Mei Jun took a deep breath and translated Billy's words, slowly and quietly.

Suddenly Mr. Hu smiled. It was a very weird smile, asymmetrical and creepy. He raised a hand to his shirt pocket and pulled out a piece of gray cloth. Billy immediately recognized it as a torn scrap from an AFMEC uniform.

Mr. Hu said one or two sentences in Chinese. His expression was bold. Predatory.

Mei Jun turned to Billy with wide eyes. "Mr. Hu says a villager found this on a rooftop near the center of town. Someone was up there this morning. Someone who broke a drainpipe off the side of a building."

Billy swallowed hard. Mr. Hu smiled another creepy smile and added a final brief sentence.

"Someone," said Mei Jun, "who looked a lot like you."

CHAPTER 15

Now it was Billy who felt trapped. Mr. Hu's creepy grin made him uncomfortable, but not nearly as uncomfortable as Mei Jun's accusing stare. *If you've got anything to get off your chest,* her eyes seemed to say, *now's the time to do it.*

"I was investigating," said Billy. "That's part of my job."

Mei Jun leaned forward and spoke quietly but forcefully. "I'm pretty sure your job doesn't include breaking things, then not telling anyone about it."

"Okay, what about that PA system I found up there?" Billy turned to Mr. Hu, trying to get back in command of the interview. "See if Mr. Hu can explain that."

Mei Jun gave Billy a suspicious squint, then translated Billy's question.

After a moment Mr. Hu answered calmly and without hesitation. "It's a warning system for the fire department. Newly installed just last week. They're quite common now. You'll find them all across China."

"But . . ." Billy ran a hand through his hair. Things weren't supposed to be like this. Mr. Hu was supposed to be confessing by now.

"But what?" Mei Jun was stony faced, much more on Mr. Hu's side of things than Billy's.

"Okay, well, what about the calligraphy? Tell him to write the characters. If he's the real Mr. Hu, he should be able to write those characters."

"*If* he's the *real* Mr. Hu?" Mei Jun looked at Billy as if he'd totally gone off the deep end. "Billy, you're not even making sense anymore."

"Yeah, well how do we know this guy's who he says he is? He could be anybody."

"Billy, this is the real Mr. Hu. There's an old newspaper article about him back at the temple. With a photo." She stared at Billy for a moment, allowing the words to sink in. "It's him. That's all there is to it."

"But . . . ," Billy said, suddenly unsure of the evidence he'd uncovered, or even if it counted as evidence at all. ". . . The Chinese characters. Why won't he write them?"

Mei Jun sighed and shook her head slowly back and forth. "Billy, if you don't have any more creatch-related questions, I suggest you apologize to Mr. Hu about the broken drainpipe and wrap this interview up as quickly as possible."

Billy stared at the tabletop.

I blew it. Mr. Hu's not going to give up anything else tonight.

Billy had to back off. "Tell him AFMEC will have that drainpipe repaired. I'll see to it personally."

"And what else should I tell him?" asked Mei Jun with a knowing glance.

"Tell him I'm . . . uh, you know . . . sorry."

Mei Jun translated Billy's apology—presumably without the "uh, you know." Mr. Hu graciously accepted it. Billy and Mei Jun finished their tea and excused themselves. As soon as they were back on the streets of Huaqing, Billy decided to risk letting Mei Jun in on his theory about Jarrid Glurrik. It suddenly seemed terribly important to get her back on his side. He needed her to understand that he wasn't crazy. That the weird interview questions, the sneaking around, the broken drainpipe, all this stuff had reasoning and logic behind it.

"Mei Jun, you're not from Huaqing, right?"

"No. Never been here until last week."

"Have you noticed anything strange about the people here?"

"Strange?"

"They're all acting very suspiciously. The children we saw this morning. Mr. Hu. Everyone. When they talk it's never spontaneous. There's always a long pause. Like they're reciting something instead of just saying the first thing that comes to mind."

"I know what you mean, Billy."

Great. She sees it too.

Mei Jun lowered her voice. "This village is so isolated. I think they've just developed their own way of talking."

"It's more than that, Mei Jun. These people have all been *coached* for these interviews. Everything they say has been fed to them by someone else."

"Fed to them?"

"I've been trained to recognize this stuff. Someone in this village is getting hold of these people before we do. Telling them what to say. Telling them what *not* to say."

Mei Jun's eyes widened with new understanding. "You think there's someone behind the scenes. Controlling everyone. Pulling strings."

"That's right, that's right." Billy's words bubbled forth now that he knew he had a sympathetic ear. "Mei Jun, I am *so* close to cracking this thing. With your help I can do it. I have a pretty good idea who it is: this guy named Jarrid Glurrik. It's just a matter of time before I figure out what he's up to."

Mei Jun nodded. "Go on."

"Okay, first of all, the PA system. That thing was *not* installed by the fire department, mark my words. It's way too compact, way too high-tech. I think it's something for transmitting information to the people in the village."

"What, like high-speed Internet?"

"Maybe. It's probably how Glurrik gives everyone their marching orders. Like, 'The AFMEC people are coming to interview you. Here's what you should tell them.' " Billy's mind was racing, coming up with a plan. "If we could do some kind of door-to-door search, maybe we could find receivers through the village, maybe even—"

"Billy," Mei Jun interrupted with a raised finger. "I've figured it out. I know what's going on here."

"You do?"

"Yes. It's not the first time. I've seen it before."

"You're kidding."

"It's called multiple-creatch-op stress disorder."

Billy blinked. He'd heard the phrase before, but it didn't seem to apply to the current situation at all. "You think the people of Huaqing are suffering from multiple-creatch-op stress disorder?"

"No, no." Mei Jun placed a hand on Billy's shoulder. "I think *you* are suffering from multiple-creatch-op stress disorder."

"*Me?* I'm not suf—"

"You are, Billy. You are. You've been on one too many missions this past month, and it's catching up with you. This happens to Affys a lot. You're starting to see problems that aren't really there. Go lie down, Billy. Get some rest."

I can't believe this. She really does *think I'm nuts.*

"But, Mei Jun, you said it yourself. The people in this village are acting *weird.*"

"They're mountain people, Billy. They have their own way of doing things."

Billy was speechless.

"Take it easy, Billy," said Mei Jun. "Take a break from all the sneaking around and coming up with theories. Trust me. A good night's rest. That's all you need."

Billy just stood there for a moment, staring at his feet. Then he raised his eyes to Mei Jun's and tried his best to sound casual and unconcerned. "Okay. I'll go lie down for a while."

"It'll do you a lot of good, Billy," said Mei Jun. "Help you stop worrying about things."

Billy said good night to Mei Jun and began the short walk back to the van. With every step he took, his spirits sank further. The day had started off so well, and he'd been making so much progress, but now everything had gone wildly off course somehow. He felt lost, as if he didn't know up from down or right from wrong.

Is Mei Jun right? Am I seeing suspicious stuff that's not even there?

CHAPTER 16

When Billy got back to the van he knew he had to come clean about what had happened on the roof. He told Ana all about the drainpipe and apologized for not having mentioned it earlier.

"Well, Billy," said Ana, "these things happen." She had a surprisingly sympathetic look in her eyes. "I'll have to put it in my report on the mission, you know. That can't be avoided. But I'll also point out that you later admitted your mistakes." She smiled and added, "Guys at AFMEC high command love it when Affys do that."

"Thanks, Ana," said Billy.

"Don't think you're off the hook, though," said Ana, her face hardening into a severe expression. "You've got to *really* stick to the rules from now on. One mistake like this is understandable. Two is not. I don't want to put you in line for an enforced leave, but I will if I have to."

An enforced leave. No participation in any creatch ops for ten weeks. It was bad enough to get one if you were an Affy. If you were an Affy-in-training, it was accompanied by a demotion to entry-level status. Like going all the way back to square one.

"Don't worry, Ana," said Billy. "I'll go strictly by the book from now on."

Ana nodded and stomped her feet to stay warm. "Go lie down, Billy." She checked her watch. "You've got two hours and fifty-seven minutes to rest. I'd use every second if I were you." She winked and added: "That midnight shift is the worst."

Billy took Ana's advice and grabbed some sleep in the van. After what felt like only ten minutes, Ana was shaking him awake.

"Come on, Billy. It's midnight. Your watch."

Billy sat up and rubbed his eyes. "Any blips on the creatch detector?" They had replaced the power cell and it was now in good working order. Hopefully.

"Nothing," said Ana, yawning. "That's the problem with being an Affy. It's either too much action or no action at all."

"Get some sleep, Ana. I'll see you at three."

After Ana hit the sack, Billy grabbed his glaff rifle and sat on a large rock near the front of the van. He then placed the creach detector at his feet and thought about the interviews, the evidence, and all that had happened the day before.

Billy raised his rifle and took a few imaginary shots at an imaginary creach on the other side of the bridge.

The kids. They seemed coached to me, but not to Mei Jun. It's a matter of interpretation. They sure didn't seem that frightened for kids who'd seen a rogmasher, but that could just be what Mei Jun said: mountain people have different ways of showing emotion.

Half an hour crawled by. Billy checked the creach detector periodically: nothing. Another half hour crawled by. Billy stood up, stretched his arms, and gave his neck a good crack.

What about the PA system? Is Mr. Hu telling the truth, that it's just for the fire department? I still think it's too high-tech for that. Then again, the high-speed Internet idea doesn't sound right either.

He checked the creach detector: nothing. He gazed across the bridge at the road beyond, and the woods beyond that. Water quietly gurgled under the bridge, but otherwise, all was silent.

Another thing: the kids' not knowing the song. Very strange, but how does it fit into all of this? If Jarrid Glurrik is coaching interviewees, that only explains the stiff-sounding answers I'm getting. It doesn't begin to explain why those kids didn't know the song at first, but then suddenly knew it seconds later.

Billy raised his glaff rifle and took another imaginary shot.

And Mr. Hu. If Mei Jun's seen his face in an old newspaper article, then he must be who he says he is. So why did he refuse to write the characters? It's a clue, it's got to be. The problem is I've got no idea how it fits in with all the other evidence.

Billy got up and walked a short distance from the bridge to the cliff's edge. He leaned on the cast-iron guardrail and looked out at the murky gray-black sky.

There's one more thing. Something I'm forgetting. It happened during the interview with the children. What was it?

Billy racked his brain for a good half hour but came up with nothing. Peering down at the treetops below the cliff, he horked up a nice big wad of spit.

Ffffwooopff!

He watched the glob of spittle fall down, down, down and finally vanish into the darkness.

This would be a pretty awesome place to try some bungee jumping. Too bad I don't have my cord with me.

Billy checked the creatch detector again: nothing. He turned his attention to the cliff overhanging the city. Moonlight glinted off a crack running straight across the middle of the cliff.

These people better pray they never have an earthquake. That's a fault line if I ever saw one. One good tremor and that whole cliff's gonna come down.

He checked the creatch detector again: nothing.

Then:

DEET DEET DEET DEET

Three red dots suddenly appeared on the screen out of nowhere, no more than five hundred yards from his position.

"Rogmashers. *Three* of them!"

CHAPTER 17

Billy stared into the pine trees on the other side of the bridge. He couldn't see them yet, but . . .

krrm krrm krrm

. . . he could hear them. He could definitely hear them.

"Oh, man. They're gonna be here any second. *Ana!*"

He ran over, yanked the passenger-side door open, and shook Ana awake. "Three rogmashers, Ana. Three!"

"Ngh? What?" Ana had been sound asleep.

"We've got to set up positions, Ana. Now! They're less than five hundred yards from town." Billy left Ana, ran to the back of the van, and started pulling out additional weaponry.

"Five hundred yards?" Ana stumbled out of the front seat, rubbing her eyes. *"Five hundred yards?"* She was awake now.

Awake enough to be angry. "Why did you wait so long to tell me?"

krrm krrm krrm

They were getting closer by the second.

"I *didn't* wait! Your stupid piece-of-*junk* creach detector sat there doing nothing—*nothing!*—until they were right outside of town."

"That's . . . impossible." Ana joined Billy in preparing the weapons on the opposite side of the bridge, lining up hortch grenades and loading both the paragglian crossbows with fresh bolts.

"No, Ana. Impossible means something that can't happen. This happened. This happened, and here we are totally unprepared: no sandbags, no barriers, nothing!"

krrm krrm krrm

"Calm down, Billy. We can handle this. Three rogmashers. That's not so bad."

DEET DEET DEET DEET

They spun around and stared in disbelief at the creach detector: two new red dots had now appeared behind the first three.

Five.

"Oh, man, we are *so* going to get massacred here."

"No, we aren't," said Ana as she grabbed both paragglian

crossbows and ran down the road toward the woods. "We can't wait until they get to the bridge. We've got to start hitting them as soon as they come out into the open. We'll use the bridge as a fallback position."

Billy grabbed both of the glaff rifles and took off after her. They found a couple of boulders to provide cover, aimed their weapons at the forest, and waited.

KRRRRM KRRRRM KRRRRM

They didn't have to wait very long. The first two rogmashers marched out of the woods just seconds later: one tall, the other shorter and fat. These two were, if anything, even uglier than the rogmasher they'd encountered earlier in the woods.

BRAM BRAM

Billy struck the big one twice in the chest, sending it stumbling backward.

BRAM

He blasted the shorter one in the gut, then grabbed the other glaff rifle. By switching between the two rifles, he could cut down on the time needed to reheat the glaffurious oxide chambers.

As Billy prepared for his next shots, Ana dashed into position, took careful aim, and shot a paragglian bolt straight up at the bigger rogmasher.

fwissshhh

BOOOOOOOAM!

An orange fireball erupted just beneath the rogmasher's jaw.

Bull's-eye!

The rogmasher staggered backward, its knees buckling, then . . .

THRRUMMM

. . . crashed to the ground, the pulsating paragglian bolt planted squarely under its chin.

"Nice shot, Ana!"

"We're not done yet, Billy," cried Ana. "Keep firing! The others will be here any second!"

BRAM BRAM BRAM

Billy's next three shots sent the shorter rogmasher reeling back, disoriented. It dropped to its knees. Ana ran in and fired another paragglian bolt straight into the underside of its chin. The rogmasher groaned, then collapsed into the middle of the road. Its massive arms flopped to the ground, then lay still.

Something's wrong here, thought Billy. *This is too easy.*

The last three rogmashers lumbered out of the woods. Two of them were carrying boulders.

Billy and Ana fell back closer to the bridge, then renewed fire. Billy was able to knock the two boulder carriers back with blasts from his glaff rifle, but the third broke through and plodded forward.

"Don't let him get across that bridge, Billy!" cried Ana as she struggled to reload her crossbows. "Do whatever it takes!"

Billy ran as fast as he could, a glaff rifle in each hand. He decided to stand his ground right in the middle of the bridge as the rogmasher approached.

BRAM BRAM BRAM

   BRAM BRAM BRAM

Three shots from each of the glaff rifles slowed the rogmasher slightly, but this one was tougher than the others. After a moment's pause it was on the move again.

Billy tossed his glaff rifles to one side and made a run for the rogmasher's leg. He pounced on its foot and started climbing, shinnying up its calf as if he were going up a tree.

GYYOOOOOAARR

The enraged beast took a swat at Billy with one of its massive fists, but Billy crouched, leaped, and hurled himself from one rogmasher leg to the other. He landed just above the knee, caught his breath, and kept climbing.

"Billy!" Ana cried in dismay. "Are you out of your mind?"

"I guess we're about to find out!"

Billy scaled the rogmasher's belly and chest. Years of rock climbing back in Indiana had prepared him for making steep ascents with nothing but his bare hands and an awful lot of willpower. As for climbing something that was lurching from

side to side, howling furiously, and attempting to squash him with both of its eight-foot-wide palms . . . well, this was definitely a first.

When Billy reached the rogmasher's shoulder, he grabbed hold of a tuft of scraggly hair and, unhooking a hortch grenade from his belt, yanked on the hair with all his might.

GGYYOOOOOOAARRR

As soon as the rogmasher opened its mouth for a deafening roar, Billy pulled the pin on the hortch grenade and threw it straight down the rogmasher's throat. He then zipped down the rogmasher's back, sliding like a snowboarder (minus both the snow and the board).

When he reached the ground, he looked up just in time to see the rogmasher double over in gastric pain. It belched, long and loud, then:

PHOOOOOM

The grenade went off, sending the rogmasher toppling to the ground. Its head hit the side of the bridge, crushing a guardrail as if it were a piece of tinfoil.

Billy turned, panting, to check on Ana's progress. She could hardly have done any better: a fourth rogmasher was down, with yet another direct hit to the underside of the chin. The last of the five was in full retreat, lumbering off into the woods on all fours.

The next thing Billy heard was the sound of applause. There, on the other side of the bridge, stood dozens of Huaqing's citizens. They'd seen the whole battle and were now treating Billy and Ana to the best standing ovation they could manage. Mei Jun stepped out from among them and offered both Ana and Billy a grateful handshake.

"Amazing!" she said, her eyes open wide in admiration. "I've seen Affys in action before, but I've never seen anything like this. Incredible!"

One by one the citizens of Huaqing stepped forward to add their thanks, and before long Billy and Ana were surrounded by a throng of Chinese men, women, and children, all showering them with gratitude. *"Xie xie, nimen,"* they kept saying again and again. *"Xie xie!"* Billy recognized it as the Mandarin phrase for thank you.

Billy and Ana had done it. They'd defended Huaqing from a full-scale attack by five—*five!*—rogmashers. Billy should have been elated. But he wasn't. Not by a long shot.

It was too easy. Way too easy. It's like the rogmashers were deliberately allowing themselves to be picked off. Something seriously weird is going on around here. But what is it?

CHAPTER 18

The people of Huaqing announced that they would prepare a huge morning feast to honor the heroes in their midst. Billy and Ana, using Mei Jun as translator, tried to persuade them to abandon the idea.

"We have to stay here near the bridge to keep watch," said Ana. "We want to be sure the rogmashers are really gone and not regrouping for another attack."

"That's right," said Billy. "This is no time for letting down our guard."

Mei Jun translated their words into Chinese. Mr. Hu would not hear a word of their objections.

"Mr. Hu says they'll make it an open-air feast," said Mei Jun. "Right here by the bridge. You won't have to leave your posts."

In the end Billy and Ana had no choice but to sit by the bridge and let them proceed with their plans. All through the night the villagers prepared their extravagant meal. Folding tables and chairs were set up. Dishes of steaming hot delicacies were brought out, one by one, and artfully arranged on the tabletops. All the while the hooded beggar played his erhu, creating a strange sound that was—no denying it—not particularly pleasing to the ear.

When Ana tried to put a call through to AFMEC to request help with cleanup operations, she found the signal blocked again.

"Ana, there is something *really* strange going on here," said Billy. "Someone's messing with our equipment."

"Slow down, Billy. We're in the mountains, remember?" Ana pointed at the huge overhang of rock looming above Huaqing.

"Okay, well, what about your creatch detector? First it runs out of juice on a fresh power cell. Then it fails to alert us to incoming creatches until it's almost too late."

"You may have something there," said Ana, pausing to give the idea serious consideration. "But it's an older model. Could be it just needs to be replaced."

"All right, Ana. Let's say I'm wrong about the equipment. That still doesn't explain why the people in this village act as if creatches aren't even a big deal to them. Look." Billy pointed to the bodies of the fallen rogmashers, masses of flies swarming over them in the early morning sun. "Not one person from the village has gone over to check out those bodies. Not one."

"Billy, Mei Jun ordered them all to stay away from the bodies. It's standard Affy procedure in China, I thought you knew that."

She was right. There had been an outbreak of disease after a creatch op in the early fifties. AFMEC insisted it had nothing to do with creatches, but the Chinese government had instituted the so-called no contact policy anyway.

"All right. All right. Here's the big one." Billy took a deep breath and pointed at Ana with both index fingers, as if trying to beam the logic of his argument straight into her. "It was too easy to take down those rogmashers. *Way* too easy. How long did it take? Ten minutes? Fifteen?"

"Billy, those rogmashers were not *easy* to take down."

"They left their weak spots *totally* unguarded. Like boxers who'd been paid to throw the match."

"You're exaggerating, Billy," said Ana. "They were a bit clumsy, yes, but they were highly aggressive. I see no evidence of a thrown fight."

Is she right? Is this all in my head?

Billy stood up and let out a long sigh.

Maybe she is. I just don't know anymore.

"Can I take a break?"

"Please do," said Ana. "You look like you really need one."

The hooded beggar went on playing his erhu, his horsehair bow screeching out the same tuneless tune, over and over and over.

I wish he'd stop playing that thing. It's driving me insane.

Soon the meal began. There were half a dozen round tables and one long rectangular table piled high with food. Ana and Billy were the guests of honor, seated in the center of it all. Villagers came by to thank them, each saying short phrases in Chinese, which Mei Jun translated faithfully at first. Eventually it became clear that they were all saying pretty much the same thing, and Mei Jun excused herself as translator, saying, "You get the idea."

The food turned out to be awful, there was no getting around it.

Man, these people can't cook. Or is it because they're isolated? Maybe Mei Jun is right.

Some dishes had no salt whatsoever; others had what tasted like a whole shakerful. Billy wasn't hungry anyway, so he just took a few nibbles and quietly slipped the rest to a stray dog near his chair. Ana ate at least twice as much as Billy, whispering to him the whole time. "It's very nice of them to do this for us, but these people *really* need to learn how to cook."

Billy kept watching the villagers, examining them for suspicious behavior. What was it about them? He couldn't put his finger on it. They were just somehow not . . . right.

If I could only bring all the info I have together, make one piece of evidence fit into the next . . .

Billy focused on Mei Jun's interactions with one of the villagers next to her. Every time she asked a question, there was always that same brief delay before the answer.

What is up with that pause?

The stray dog whined for more food.

"Pipe down, boy," said Billy, giving him a bright red chunk of barbecued pork. "I'm trying to think here."

Mei Jun asked a question.

The dog whined.

The villager answered.

Wait a minute.

Mei Jun asked another question.

The dog whined again.

The villager answered.

Wait. A. Minute.

All at once things began to fall into place. Billy understood everything: the high-tech PA system, the long delays when people answered questions. Billy turned and looked at the dog, which was still whining whenever Mei Jun asked the villager a question.

That's what I forgot to write down during the interview with the children: the whining stray dog. It's the key to the whole thing!

Billy rose from his seat.

"What are you doing?" Ana said.

"I know what's going on here, Ana," said Billy. "I'll show you. Keep an eye on the stray dog while I do this, all right?"

"The stray dog? Billy, what are you talk—"

"I know it sounds crazy, but just . . . trust me. I know what I'm doing."

He had a plan. It was risky, and if he was wrong, he'd make a fool of himself. But he wasn't wrong. He knew it.

Billy walked over to Mr. Hu. The hooded beggar stopped playing his erhu—only for a second, but long enough for Billy to notice—then resumed playing.

"Mei Jun," said Billy, "ask Mr. Hu what his favorite color is."

Mei Jun rose from her chair with a pained not-this-again look on her face. "Billy, I hardly think this is the appropriate time to—"

"Please, Mei Jun. You've got to do this for me. Two or three simple questions and this will all be over."

Mei Jun translated the question.

A pause.

The dog whined.

Mr. Hu answered. Before Mei Jun could translate, Billy called out to Ana: "Did you hear that? The dog whined, right?"

"Yeah," said Ana, a troubled look on her face. She was clearly more worried about Billy losing his mind than anything else. "What about it?"

"It's a pattern, Ana. Watch, I'll do it again." Billy turned to Mei Jun. "Ask Mr. Hu something trickier. Ask him what the ingredients are in these steamed dumplings."

Mei Jun translated the question.

A longer pause.

The dog whined.

Mr. Hu answered.

"You see how it works?" Billy said to Ana. "Question. Pause. Whine. Answer. Every time, Ana. *Every time.*"

Ana and Mei Jun exchanged worried glances. Billy knew they were thinking the same thing: multiple-creatch-op stress disorder. Big-time.

"Don't you see, Ana?" Billy pointed at the stray dog. "That dog is whining because it hears something. Something you and I can't hear. It hears messages."

"Messages?" said Ana.

"Yeah. Broadcast from that PA system I saw the other day. *Messages.*"

Ana now looked convinced that Billy had finally gone off the deep end. "You think someone's broadcasting messages . . . to the *dog*?"

"No, no, no. Not to the dog. To Mr. Hu. To everyone in this village. The dog just overhears the messages. It's all so clear. Now we just need to figure out how he hears our questions."

"He?" said Ana. "Who's he?"

"I'm about to find out, Ana." Billy circled the tables, checking under them, upsetting dishes of food. "All right, big guy," he said, as if talking to a ghost that only he could see, "I know you're listening in on all this. Just like you've been from the moment we set foot in this village."

"Billy," said Ana, "you really need to calm down. You're freaking everyone out."

"Believe me, Ana. The sooner we freak these people out, the better. They're all working for the same guy." Billy was fishing through a potted plant near one of the tables. "There's a microphone here somewhere, Ana. That's how he hears our questions and feeds everyone their answers."

"Look, Billy. That's enough. Sit down and take a break."

Billy suddenly turned in the direction of Mei Jun. "Mei Jun. Of course. She's always with us when we talk to the villagers. She's bugged."

Mei Jun shot Ana a frightened look. Was Billy accusing *her* of something?

"Billy—" said Ana. But it was too late. Billy had already dashed between the tables to where Mei Jun was standing.

"It's the jade brooch you're wearing, Mei Jun. The one Mr. Hu gave you. There's a microphone in it." Billy leaned down and spoke in the direction of the jade flower. "Isn't there? How am I coming through, man? Can you hear me loud and clear?"

"Billy!" said Ana, rising from her chair. "That's enough. You promised me we were going to do things by the book. Now stop this craziness and sit down."

"Stop?" said Billy to Ana. "We can't *afford* to stop now, Ana. We can't stop until we find out who's *behind* all this." He turned from Mei Jun and crossed back to Mr. Hu. Billy was already way past the point of no return, but he still had to swallow hard and brace himself for what he was about to do.

Here we go.

Billy roughly grabbed hold of Mr. Hu's shirt collar with both hands. He pulled Mr. Hu up from his chair, toward his own face, until their noses nearly touched.

"Who do you work for?"

Now the hooded beggar's erhu went silent altogether.

Ana was on her feet and dashing between the tables to break things up. "Billy! Let go of him! Now!"

"No, Ana." Billy pulled Mr. Hu farther away from the chair he'd been sitting on. His surprisingly light body put up little resistance. "Not until he tells who he's working for."

"Billy, I *order* you to let go of him."

"I don't take orders from you, Ana."

"Yes, you do. This is *my* creach op, Billy."

Yours?

"I didn't want to tell you, but it's true. It's my creatch op, and you are under my direct supervision. Now let go of him."

If I'm wrong about this . . .

Billy gritted his teeth and tightened his grip on Mr. Hu's collar.

I'm not wrong. I'm not.

"I've got proof, Ana. Proof that I'm not just making this all up."

Billy turned Mr. Hu's head to one side and looked into his ear. If he was right, there would be a listening device there, one that made the high-pitched messages audible to human ears. But when Billy gazed into Mr. Hu's ear canal he saw no listening device whatsoever. What he did see sent a chill down his spine.

Mucus. Green, pulsating mucus.

No. Way.

"Okay, Billy," said Ana. "Let's see this proof. Because if you can't justify any of this, I'm taking you off the job. You leave me no choice."

"He's not human, Ana." Billy looked around at the villagers. "None of them are."

There was murmuring among the villagers, murmuring in a language that was definitely *not* Chinese.

A voice rose above the others, high-pitched and raspy: *"Zizziss! Siffiss niss fississ!"* It sounded like an announcement, or a command. It had come from the mouth of the hooded beggar.

All at once Mr. Hu's face began to change. The skin color turned blue, then green. The nose vanished altogether. The eyes enlarged and slid back to the sides of the head. The mouth drooped and melted into a wide, toadlike frown. Within seconds he had gone from an old Chinese man to something resembling a gargantuan salamander.

Ana gasped. Mei Jun looked like she was about to faint.

"Ziiissssssss!" The newt creature wriggled out of his clothing and leaped across the ground on all fours, bounding from place to place with agile slimy legs. Billy stood there wide-eyed, stunned by his own discovery. He knew something strange was going on in Huaqing, but he hadn't counted on this.

A great hissing went out from the crowd as one by one the people of Huaqing mutated into green-skinned creatures all but indistinguishable from one another.

Creatches. They're forest creatches, all of them!

CHAPTER 19

Within seconds every last villager had changed into a creatch.

"Vizziss!" The hooded beggar pointed with an outstretched finger as he hissed his orders. *"Fiffiss niss!"*

The amphibianlike beings surrounded Billy, Ana, and Mei Jun in a flash, latching onto their arms and legs with lightning speed. There was little point in resisting. They were so drastically outnumbered by the forest creatches it was impossible to even move, much less put up a fight.

"Impressive," said the hooded beggar, rising from his chair. The voice was deep and authoritative. "Your powers of observation are remarkable, young man." The hood was now drawn back enough to reveal an old man's wrinkled face framed by neatly combed silver-white hair. Pale blue eyes squinted beneath eyebrows so thin and wispy they were hardly there at all. A cropped white beard and mustache surrounded a wide, thin-lipped mouth.

"Glurrik," whispered Billy. "Jarrid Glurrik."

"Ahh, you know my name, do you?" The old man stepped forward, inspecting Billy and Ana as if they were captured insects. "I feared the younger generation had not been told of me. But I made quite an impression on your elders, didn't I?"

"Where are the people of Huaqing?" asked Billy. "What have you done with them?"

"You needn't worry about them," said Glurrik. "They are alive. We creatch supremacists are not interested in killing humans. If we were to do that, who would serve as our slaves when the day of triumph arrives?" He smiled and brought his face closer to Billy's. "And that day is coming soon, my friend. Make no mistake. Creatches are superior life-forms. Better adapted to survival than we frail humans. That's why I cast my lot with them."

"Jallavirms," said Ana, staring angrily at the slimy green creatures restraining her. "Chameleonating forest creatches."

That's why they were able to hear Glurrik's messages, thought Billy. *Forest creatches have powers of hearing way beyond humans.*

"They did a *very* good job, you have to admit," said Glurrik. "You had no idea they weren't real. Why, even a native Chinese"— he waved a hand in the direction of Mei Jun—"couldn't tell the

difference." He trained his eyes on Billy and addressed him with grudging respect. "If not for your persistence, I'd have pulled it all off quite nicely. Still, I'm glad you were sent on this mission, boy. You've done a commendable job of troubleshooting my plan."

Glurrik paced back and forth, speaking his thoughts aloud while counting on long spindly fingers. "I'll have to rid the other villages of stray dogs, for starters."

Other villages? He's got this whole operation set up in other places besides Huaqing!

"And we'll have to restrict Affy access to villagers. There's no way of anticipating illogical requests like the ones you cooked up." Glurrik sneered at Billy. "It was just dumb luck that I was

able to recall that silly children's song you asked for. And as for calligraphy . . . well, jallavirms are good at looking and sounding like human beings, but their fine motor skills leave much to be desired."

"You're going to do this all over China, aren't you?" said Billy. "Lure Affys into fake creach ops, then ambush them when they least expect it."

Glurrik stopped pacing long enough to smile at Billy.

"You make it sound so simple. You have no idea how hard it is to train rogmashers and jallavirms to do one's bidding. Or how many years I've worked on such problems as jamming Affy viddy-fone transmissions and inducing failure in creach detectors. With all that work it would be folly to restrict my activities to China. I've got operations like this set up all across the globe, ready to be unleashed at my word."

Glurrik patted Billy on the cheek. "Such the sleuth you are. And to think you're not even a full-fledged Affy. It's a real tragedy that they didn't at least welcome you into the fold before sending you to your death."

We've seen too much. He's not going to let us out of here.

Billy struggled against the jallavirms, but they held him firmly. "This won't go unnoticed," he said. "AFMEC will figure out what you're up to. No matter what you do with us."

Glurrik grinned. "Admirable faith, little man. Utterly misplaced, but admirable all the same. It's really a pity you're not on my side. I could use a blindly dedicated minion like you."

Glurrik turned his back to Billy, took several strides toward the bridge, and pointed at the van. "Time to be rid of this. Don't want anyone escaping."

Glurrik pushed a button on a remote control he was holding. After a second . . .

PHOOOOOOM!

. . . a spectacular explosion erupted beneath the van, lifting it fully five feet into the air before sending it crashing to the ground. It landed on its side, weaponry spilling from its rear doors.

"Alas, you've brought this on yourself, you see," said Glurrik. "I didn't intend for you to die here in Huaqing. Quite the contrary. You were meant to return to AFMECopolis victorious, blissfully unaware of my deceptions."

Glurrik continued walking as he spoke, crossing the bridge that led out of Huaqing.

"It's over now. All the evidence must be destroyed, including the three of you. Don't go to your graves thinking you foiled my plot, though. You merely exposed the flaws in my test run." He chuckled. "Thanks to you, the success of my future efforts is all but guaranteed."

Glurrik stopped and turned for one last word.

"Put up your very best fight," he said. "I expect nothing less from you." Then he continued walking until he vanished into the woods south of town.

CHAPTER 20

Several minutes later the jallavirms released Billy, Ana, and Mei Jun and scurried out of Huaqing at lightning speed. Within seconds the three of them were the only ones left in the village. Billy and Ana ran to salvage whatever weaponry they could from the van. Most of it had been severely damaged. Fortunately Ana had taken the precaution of creating a stash outside the van, and this weaponry was unscathed.

"He's setting us up for one final battle, a battle he knows we can't win," said Billy as he loaded hortch grenades into a wooden crate. "We've got to get across that bridge. We'll be sitting ducks in Huaqing. He knows it's a dead end once you're on this side of the bridge. That's the only reason he chose this town in the first place: it's a perfect laboratory for his big experiment."

They grabbed as much weaponry as they could carry—Mei

Jun included—and began making their way across the bridge. Just as they reached the other side, they heard a sickeningly familiar sound.

Krrm krrm krrm

"Rogmashers," said Ana. "A lot of them, by the sound of it."

"I knew it," said Billy. "He's had them waiting in the woods the whole time, ready to cut us off."

Sure enough, as they made their way around a bend in the road, they saw no fewer than seven rogmashers already in place, blocking the way out of town. A growing battalion of rogmashers was already joining them, emerging from the forest by twos and threes.

"He's got a whole army of them!" said Ana as she and Billy and Mei Jun came to a stop.

"Of course he does," said Billy. "That's the whole plan, isn't it? Bring the Affys in for a creatch op. Fool them into thinking they've succeeded. Then bring on the *real* threat when they're least prepared to defend themselves. He'll get AFMEC's best and brightest right where he wants them, then: wham! If he pulls it off, he could gut the organization's ranks in a single day."

Krrrrm krrrrm krrrrm

The rogmashers were beginning to march forward up the road to Huaqing. There were now more than a dozen of them.

Mei Jun was beginning to look ill. The color had gone from

her face. She grabbed Billy and Ana by the arms. "We've got to get back to the village! Hide inside one of the buildings!"

"We'll go back to the village, all right," said Billy as the three of them turned around and began running back to the bridge, "but we're not going to hide anywhere. Those rogmashers will flatten every building in town by the time this is over."

"So what else can we do?" said Ana. "There's no way we can take on all those rogmashers by ourselves."

"We're going to have to at least try," said Billy. "I say we go to the temple and make our last stand there. The rogmashers will come in for the kill. We hit them with everything we've got.

If we lose the fight, we lose the fight. But at least we'll take a few of Glurrik's thugs down with us."

"That plan," said Ana, "is about as close to suicidal as I've ever heard."

"You like it, eh?"

"Love it."

Billy, Ana, and Mei Jun dashed across the bridge and began rummaging through what was left of the equipment in the van.

"Billy, I'll need every last one of those paragglian bolts. Where did you put the extras?"

Billy retrieved the scuffed-up case. Ana squinted at it, confused. "That's not right. Paragglian bolts come in a smaller case than that."

KRRRM KRRRM KRRRRM

There was no time to discuss it. "Come on, we've got to get to the temple and set up shop." Billy grabbed the case in one arm and a crate of hortch grenades in the other. Mei Jun and Ana split the paragglian crossbows and glaff rifles between them. Then the three of them made their way through the streets of Huaqing to the temple.

Mei Jun led them to a balcony near the roof where they

would have a clear view of any approaching rogmashers. Looking across the rooftops, they saw more of the towering beasts emerge from the forest on the other side of the bridge. The rogmasher batallion numbered twenty in all: enough to destroy even a seasoned crew of Affys, to say nothing of a pair of its youngest members and their civilian assistant.

Billy's mind was racing as he laid out the modest array of paragglian crossbows, glaff rifles, and hortch grenades they'd managed to bring with them. There was no getting around it. Glurrik had worked out all the angles: No way of calling in backup. No transport out of town. Too little weaponry for the job. Way too little manpower.

"Ana," said Billy as the first of the rogmashers began marching across the bridge, "how many rogmashers do you think you can take down with that crossbow?"

"Plenty," said Ana. "I've got some bad news for you, though. Whatever's in that case, it's not paragglian bolts. You grabbed the wrong thing, Billy. I'm sorry, but you did."

KRRRRM KRRRM KRRRRM

The rogmashers were making their way through the village, some of them stomping right through the roofs of houses on their way to the temple. They were taking their time, secure in the knowledge that they had their prey cornered. Even moving slowly, though, they'd be at the doorstep of the temple within minutes.

Billy unlocked the case and threw it open. There was nothing inside but a heavy khaki-colored bundle of cloth, with straps and cords hanging off it.

A parachute. I grabbed a freakin' parachute instead of the ammo.

He closed the case and saw at once that the scuffed-up label that he'd thought was PARA and the first part of a *G* was, in fact, half of PARACHUTE, not PARAGGLIAN BOLTS.

Oh, man, are we hosed. We are so hosed.

"There are three spare bolts on the underside of one of the crossbows," said Ana. "That's it. That's all we've got."

The rogmashers were already beginning to close in on the temple.

Billy and Ana kept up as steady a volley of fire as they could, blasting the rogmashers with their glaff rifles and hurling hortch grenades whenever possible. There was no stopping the onslaught, though. The rogmashers were going to reach the temple eventually.

There's got to be another way out of Huaqing.

Billy's mind raced. He tried to picture the map Mei Jun had shown them on the table the day before.

The village. The road. The temple. The . . .

. . . dotted line.

The dotted line. It led away from the temple and over the side of the cliff. It was a footpath. It had to be.

Billy turned to Ana. "Give me five seconds. I've got to check something out."

Billy climbed a support beam and crawled to the highest reaches of the temple roof. When he got to the top, he had a clear view of the narrow strip of land between the temple and the cliff. A crude stone wall had been constructed at the edge where the ground began to drop off. There, in the very spot on the map where the dotted line had been drawn, was a gap in the wall, and crumbling steps curving down and away.

Yes!

Billy slid back down the roof and jumped to the balcony.

"Mei Jun, you need to get out of here before things really heat up," he said.

Mei Jun shook her head. "I can't leave you two alone like this. I've got to help out somehow."

"We'll be leaving too," said Billy, "just a little after you. Now listen. There's a trail there at the very edge of the cliff. I saw it marked on the map you showed us the other day. It goes about half a mile straight north out of the village. After that it's going to get awfully steep—and who knows what kind of condition it's in—but at least it'll get you out of Huaqing and maybe even all the way down to the valley. Ana and I will stay here and see how many more rogmashers we can take out. Then we'll meet you on the trail."

"But, Billy," said Mei Jun, "I can't leave you and Ana here by yourselves battling so many rogmashers. It's far too dangerous."

"The rogmashers are dangerous, all right," said Billy. "That's why we can't afford to leave any more of them under Glurrik's control than we have to. If we're lucky, Ana and I will be able to cut their number by half."

Not with only three paragglian bolts between us, but Mei Jun doesn't need to know that. The main thing is to get her out of here. Ana and I will be able to save our own skins when the going gets rough.

Ana put a hand on Mei Jun's shoulder. "Billy's right. We can't let Glurrik get away from this with his rogmasher army intact." She gave Mei Jun a farewell hug. "Don't worry about us. We've got enough ammo to defend ourselves. More than enough."

"I can't do this," said Mei Jun. "You're going to get yourselves killed if you stay here."

"Ten minutes more," said Billy. "Then we're out of here. We can outrun any rogmashers that come after us. They may be strong, but they're slowpokes when it comes to a footrace."

Mei Jun sighed and nodded. "Okay. Ten minutes," she said. "Then you two get your little Affy butts on that trail!"

"Mine is an Affy butt-in-training," said Billy with a grin. "But it appreciates the promotion, I'm sure."

Mei Jun rolled her eyes and turned to Ana. "Be careful, Ana. No more heroics for you two. You've done more than enough for one creatch op."

"No more heroics," said Ana. "I promise."

"All right, then. *Zai jian,* my friends. I'll see you both on the trail." She turned and faced them one more time before climbing across the roof and out of sight. *"Ten minutes."*

CHAPTER 21

As soon as Mei Jun was gone, the final assault of the rogmashers began in earnest. Within seconds all twenty of the beasts were less than five hundred yards from the gate of the temple, closing the gaps between one another, forming a terrifying wall of heads, chests, and massive leathery arms.

"No more heroics, eh?" said Billy as he unleashed several blasts of glaffurious oxide.

"I was crossing my fingers when I said that."

"You must have been crossing your fingers *and* toes when you said we had plenty of ammo," said Billy. "Man oh man. We must be insane."

"We're Affys, Billy. Being insane is right there in the job description." Ana had one paragglian bolt loaded and the other two at her side. To even have a chance of hitting one of the beasts on the underside of the chin, she'd have to wait until the whole battalion was nearly on top of them. In the meantime, she joined Billy in keeping up a constant barrage of fire with the glaff rifles.

The rogmashers were soon within a hundred yards of the gates. They smashed buildings and uprooted utility poles as they went, clearing the battlefield in advance of the final attack. Several of them hurled boulders, tearing holes through the roof of the temple and shaking the pillars.

Billy tossed hortch grenade after hortch grenade, knocking one or two of the rogmashers back on its heels for a moment, only to find others stepping in to take their place.

"They're almost in range," said Ana, dropping her glaff rifle and picking up the loaded paragglian crossbow. "I should be able to take one of them down before we go. Maybe two."

"I don't know how much longer this balcony will hold, Ana," said Billy as he threw a hortch grenade into the crowd of rogmashers that now stood at the very gates of the temple. "You peg even one of those suckers and I say it's time to roll."

"Deal," said Ana as she took aim at the rogmasher nearest the gate.

"Let's see if I can't get that guy to expose his weak spot."

BRAM BRAM BRAM

Billy's glaff blasts struck the rogmasher three times: once in each shoulder and once in the chest.

GGYYOOOOOAARRRR

As it roared, the furious beast tilted its head back for a fraction of a second. Ana didn't waste the opportunity.

Fffffffssssshhhhhh

POOOOAAMM!

Red-orange fire erupted from the rogmasher's chin. Its knees gave out and it crashed to the ground in a cloud of dust and flying concrete.

There was little to celebrate. The remaining rogmashers had broken through the temple walls and were now within striking distance of the temple itself. Several of them were already beginning to tear the roof to pieces. One was battering the balcony's support beams with its fists, shattering them like candy canes. Another raised both hands in the air and, with a single blow, obliterated the stairway leading up to the balcony.

"That's it, Ana," Billy cried. "We've gotta bail!"

Clutching their weapons, the two of them climbed from the balcony to the roof, then scrambled up to the top.

"See the trail?" asked Billy as he took a few parting blasts at a rogmasher with his glaff rifle. "If we can just get down there and—"

"Billy," said Ana. "We're in trouble."

Billy turned to point out the gap in the wall but found himself pointing instead at a collapsed section of the cliff. One of the boulders thrown by a rogmasher had destroyed the upper portions of the trail not long after Mei Jun left, creating a sheer drop-off where the trail used to be. There would be no escaping on foot for Billy and Ana. They were trapped. End of story.

The roof began to shake. Rogmashers had now encircled the temple completely and were battering away at it, bit by bit. Their horrid, twisted blue-gray faces were now so close Billy could see the saliva dripping from their lips. Ana and Billy huddled together at the very crest of the roof, their zone of safety growing smaller by the second.

That's it. We're trapped. We're completely trapped.

Billy fired desperately at any rogmasher he could hit. Ana shot off one of the two remaining paragglian bolts, but it failed to reach its target. What did it matter, anyway? At this point, they were just postponing the inevitable. The end was coming. It would all be over in a matter of minutes.

Billy racked his brain for a solution. There had to be a way out. They couldn't just sit here until the rogmashers killed them. He stared longingly at the valley below, wishing they could somehow jump off the cliff and magically fly away to safety.

What am I, nuts? We jump off that cliff and we'll break every last bone in our bodies.

Unless . . .

"The parachute!" Billy spun around. There it was, half out of its case, tucked into the corner of the balcony, or what little of the balcony remained. Billy thrust his glaff rifle into Ana's hands. "I've got to get that parachute. It's our only way out of this."

Billy slid down the roof and leaped down to the balcony. He was now well within arm's length of at least three rogmashers. They roared and raised their fists to smash him into oblivion.

Billy rolled across the balcony.

HHHWWWAAAMMM

One of the rogmasher's ten-foot-wide fists crashed down just inches from Billy's head, sending wood and iron flying. Billy somersaulted, grabbed one of the parachute's straps, threw it over his shoulder, and bolted back across the balcony to the roof.

THHHAAAAAMMMMM

A second fist blew away the balcony altogether just as Billy leaped and hurled himself to the edge of the roof with every ounce of strength he had. The enraged roars of rogmashers blended into a deafening, furious chorus. Rogmasher fists rained down on all sides as Billy dodged one, then another, then another.

Have to get back to Ana.

FFWWUUUMMP

All went black. One of the rogmashers had cupped its enormous hands and closed them around Billy like a child catching a grasshopper.

No!

Billy felt himself rising, heard the air whistling through the rogmasher's fingers. Then the huge, leathery palms of the rogmasher began to close in on him.

It's gonna crush me!

Billy thrust out his arms and legs, trying to keep the two enormous palms apart, but it was hopeless. He was caught inside a massive, flesh-and-blood vise, and nothing could stop it from clamping shut.

Billy's arms and legs gave out. Within seconds there was no space left between him and the palms of the rogmasher. He could do nothing but lie there, arms at his sides, and wait as the breath got squeezed out of him.

Then, somewhere beyond the rogmasher's hands . . .

Fffffffffsssssssshhhhh

POOOOOOOAAAAAAAAMMMMMM!

Orange-yellow light poured between the rogmasher's fingers as its hands opened and dropped Billy to the rooftop. Billy turned just in time to see the towering beast—a glowing paragglian bolt protruding from the underside of its chin—reel backward and collapse into the south wing of the temple.

Billy scrambled up the rooftop to where Ana stood, her paragglian crossbow still clutched firmly in her hands.

"Ana, you rock," he said as he strapped the parachute on with trembling hands, "you really do."

"I couldn't let that guy flatten you, Billy," said Ana, smiling. "You're thin enough as it is."

The eighteen remaining rogmashers pounded forward, plowing into the temple on all sides, tearing it to pieces as if it were a house of cards. Roof tiles whirled into the air. Pieces of concrete shot in all directions. Billy and Ana were soon standing on an island of intact roof tiles less than forty feet in diameter.

"We've got to jump!" cried Ana. "Now!"

"No," said Billy as he raised his glaff rifle. "One last shot."

"It's a waste of time," said Ana. "Let's just jump and get it over with."

"Trust me, Ana," said Billy as he aimed the glaff rifle, not at any of the rogmashers, but at the vast cliff overlooking what little remained of the village of Huaqing. "This will *not* be a waste of time."

BRAM BRAM BRAM

The blasts of glaffurious oxide struck the overhang of stone in three separate spots along the fault line Billy had noticed the night before.

bbbrrrrrruuuuummmmMMMMMMMMM

The rogmashers raised their heads in horror as the vast ceiling of stone above them began to crack, crumble, and fall to pieces right on top of them.

"*Now* we jump," said Billy. Ana grabbed on to Billy and the two of them dove from the temple. All was a blur as they cleared the edge of the cliff and—for a terrifying few seconds—went into a free fall that threatened to send them plunging to their deaths in a forest of pine trees hundreds of yards below.

Here's hoping AFMEC keeps its parachutes in good repair, thought Billy as he pulled the cord.

FFFFWWWHHHHHOOOOOOOSSSHHhhhh

The parachute rocketed Billy and Ana upward as it opened, shooting them into the sky as if they'd been fired out of a cannon. All at once they were treated to a dazzling aerial view of the valley on one side and the collapsing cliff on the other. The rogmashers roared in dismay as an avalanche of stone thundered down on top of them. Within minutes the disintegrating cliff turned Huaqing into a vast graveyard for Glurrik's rogmasher army, burying them under tons and tons of stone and sand.

"Nice, Billy," said Ana as they floated down and away to safety. "*Messy.* But nice."

CHAPTER 22

"So let me get this straight, Clikk. You intended to save the village of Huaqing by completely destroying it?"

It was a day later. Billy and Ana were in a small fluorescent-lit office in AFMECopolis, going through the first of what promised to be many debriefing sessions following the completed creatch op in China. They were being interviewed by a balding, bespectacled man who strongly disapproved of Billy's parting shot at the cliff. It was against the rules. This guy liked rules.

"No, see, Huaqing was pretty much toast already at that point." Billy had already explained the sequence of events a half-dozen times and it somehow sounded worse with every fresh attempt. "The rogmashers had totally leveled the place."

"Oh, well, I'd better make a note of that," said Balding Guy.

"Agent García and Agent-in-Training Clikk . . ." He said the words aloud as he scribbled them in a notebook. ". . . employed tactics that encouraged the rogmashers to completely level the village of Huaqing."

"No," said Ana. "No, it wasn't like that at all. We had no choice but to fight them in the middle of the village. There was no other—"

"That takes care of that," said Balding Guy, clicking his pen several times for no apparent reason. "Now tell me again how it was that you failed to capture Jarrid Glurrik at the end of the mission."

Billy sighed. Letting Glurrik escape unpunished was the one part of the creatch op that really nagged at him. The parachute had brought Billy and Ana down in a grassy clearing in the valley. After using their viddy-fones to call AFMEC for reinforcements—having finally escaped Glurrik's zone of communications jamming—they made their way through the woods until they found Mei Jun on the trail leading down from Huaqing. The three of them camped out on the trail until an AFMEC vehicle arrived and flew them back into the mountains to begin cleanup operations.

A subsequent search party discovered the location of the true citizens of Huaqing deep in the woods north of the village. They had been shelterless for days, trapped behind a massive barbed-wire fence, but were relatively unharmed. Glurrik was by then long gone, having returned to his own secret head-quarters, presumably to begin work on his next effort to bring AFMEC to its knees.

"Glurrik was never within our reach," said Billy. "We were restrained by the jallavirms until he was out of town."

Balding Guy raised his eyebrows. He didn't seem to buy this part of the story. Or *any* part of the story, really. "Well, I can tell you one thing, kids," he said. "Mr. Vriffnee is not going to like what he sees in my report: shoddy preparatory work, forgotten equipment, failure to recognize creach imposters, and . . ." He trained his eyes on Billy. ". . . *gross* misuse of weaponry resulting in the destruction of an entire village."

Ana was furious. "You can't put it like that."

"I already *have* put it like that, my dear."

TUNK TUNK TUNK

A knock on the door.

"That will be Agent Prachett," said Balding Guy as he rose to get the door. "You two had better brace yourselves. He's not as easygoing as I am."

Ana and Billy sank into their chairs.

But when the door opened:

"Mr. Vriffnee!"

Ana and Billy turned their heads to see none other than the prime magistrate of AFMEC standing at the door. He was wearing a tweedy brown suit and his usual thick spectacles. Billy had never seen the man smile, but today he looked particularly grim.

"What an honor, sir," said Balding Guy.

"I'll take it from here," said Mr. Vriffnee.

"M-my report, sir," said Balding Guy, offering the forms onto which he'd scribbled his notes.

"Thank you. That will be all, Agent."

"Thank *you,* sir."

K'CHAK

Mr. Vriffnee strode across the room and sat in the same chair where Balding Guy had been. He stroked his mustache and stared silently at Billy and Ana for a moment, his squinting gray-blue eyes betraying no emotion.

When he finally spoke, it was after a brief sigh. "So he got away, eh?"

"Yes, sir," said Ana. "He did."

Mr. Vriffnee nodded. "Jarrid Glurrik. Still trying to break the spine of AFMEC after all these years. Such is the determination of the creatch supremacists."

"I'm . . . sorry, sir," said Billy.

"Are you, now? Well, maybe you'd better tell me exactly what it is you're sorry for."

"I'm sorry I let Glurrik get away. Sorry I didn't recognize the forest creatches sooner. Sorry I . . ." Billy paused and lowered his gaze. ". . . I destroyed what was left of Huaqing."

Mr. Vriffnee frowned. "Well, yes, you did quite a number on that place, didn't you? Must be something in the Clikk family blood. Your father once did the very same thing to a small mining town in Montana. Did he ever tell you about that?"

"No, sir."

Mr. Vriffnee chuckled. "Ask him about it sometime. If

you want to see him really squirm." Billy smiled. When it came to making people squirm, no one knew how better than Mr. Vriffnee.

"Look, it comes down to this." Mr. Vriffnee leaned forward in his chair. "You two were faced with a creach op far more challenging than anything either of you has ever faced before. You made some missteps. Some miscalculations. And your exit from Huaqing was, shall we say, rather more *dramatic* than I would have liked."

Billy and Ana grew red in the face.

"But you defeated the foe placed before you, and you uncovered a potentially devastating plot to deceive AFMEC. Thanks to you, we will be far less likely to fall for such a scheme in the future. Taking into account the various pluses and minuses of your conduct, my final verdict on the creach op is this."

He paused for a long time, long enough to make Billy and Ana do some squirming of their own.

"Good job." Vriffnee smiled an almost imperceptible smile. "That's it. I've canceled the other three debriefing sessions that were on the schedule."

Mr. Vriffnee scooted his chair back and rose to his feet. "You two have had enough for one day."

Ana was confused. "What should we do in place of those sessions, Mr. Vriffnee?"

Mr. Vriffnee held Balding Guy's report at arm's length to read the title page. "It's Saturday." He cleared his throat. "Get outside. Have some fun."

Mr. Vriffnee threw the report into a trash can and closed the door behind him.

CHAPTER 23

On Monday morning when Billy arrived back at Piffling Elementary, he was more than ready for a quiet day at school. As a sign of appreciation for the work in China, Mr. Vriffnee had granted both Billy and Ana three days off duty, and Billy had to admit he needed the break. His arms, legs, and torso were covered with scrapes and bruises, and every muscle in his body ached from overexertion. Even after spending most of Sunday vegging out in front of the tube, an extra day or two of downtime at school was much appreciated.

When the final bell rang at the end of Monday's last class, Billy grabbed his backpack, hopped on his skateboard, and headed for Marvy Marv's, his skateboarding supplier of choice. He'd only just gotten off school property when a familiar voice called after him.

"Yo, Clikkmaster Flash!"

Nelson, thought Billy with a groan. *Leave it to him to wreck an otherwise good day.*

Nelson Skubblemeyer shuffled over to Billy, wearing his usual wannabe-trendy baggy pants and football jersey. Jake was right behind him. *Here we go.* Today Nelson looked even more ridiculous than usual, since whoever had rebleached his hair over the weekend—Jake, no doubt—had totally blown it, leaving him looking like a platinum-furred dalmatian.

"Clikkmaster, what's the big rush, my man?" Nelson pulled his shades down just enough to peer over them with his beady eyes. "If I didn't know better I'd think you were tryin' to avoid me."

"Dude," said Jake, "we got a job for you." He was wearing the same ensemble Nelson was, only three or four sizes bigger and considerably more wrinkled, as if he'd slept in it (a very real possibility, knowing Jake). He was holding a rolled-up stack of loose-leaf with red marks all over it.

"Check it out, Clikkmaster," said Nelson, nodding in the direction of the loose-leaf and pushing his shades back up in front of his eyes. "My man Jake here has a sit-uation," he added, drawing the last word out to create an unnaturally big gap between *sit* and *chewation.*

"Yeah," said Jake, as if he were clarifying something. "A situation."

"He's got this paper he wrote for Mrs. Dembinski's class," said Nelson. "I helped him rewrite it, but the lady must've been confused or something 'cause it came back with a worse grade than what he started with."

"Now it's your turn," said Jake, thrusting the paper into Billy's chest. "You get good grades. You know all about writing and stuff." He said it as if it were a disease Billy suffered from.

Billy kept his hands at his sides. Taking hold of the paper would be seen as an acceptance of Jake's demand.

How can I get this guy to back off? Permanently.

"Take it, man," said Jake, stepping to within a foot of Billy's face. Billy stopped breathing through his nose. Too late: he now had ample—and very much unwanted—evidence that Jake's snack du jour had been Cool Ranch Doritos.

"Take it," said Jake. Now the loose-leaf was unrolled and raised to within an inch of Billy's chin, like a knife to his throat.

"Clikkmaster," said Nelson. "You're a smart guy. You're not going to give Jake any trouble . . ." Nelson lowered his shades again and gave Billy a brotherly wink. ". . . are you?"

Billy took a deep breath and let it out slowly. He was so tired of backing down. He wanted to put Jake in his place, but how could he do it without breaking AFMEC rules? He couldn't. That was all there was to it.

"I'm not going to ask you again," said Jake, as if the phrase "Take it" had been a question.

"Listen, Jake," said Billy. "If I rewrite that paper for you, Mrs. Dembinski will see your writing suddenly get better overnight. Then she'll get suspicious."

Jake frowned and drew his unibrow down over his eyes. Nelson shook his head with a pained expression on his face. He cupped a hand to one side of his mouth and whispered, "Don't do this to yourself, man. You haven't seen the kind of damage Jake can do."

"Let me finish," said Billy, keeping his eyes on Jake. "See, what you need is a *series* of papers, not just one. You need a series of papers that get better and better. That way it looks like you're improving naturally."

Nelson and Jake stared and said nothing, unsure of where Billy was going with this.

"Yeah," continued Billy, raising a finger to signify that he had now hatched the perfect scheme. "What we'll do is have me start rewriting *all* your papers from now on."

Nelson did a double take worthy of a corny TV sitcom. He squinted at Billy, trying to decide if he was joking. Jake just grinned as if he'd expected Billy to cave all along.

"I'll bring this one up to a C," Billy said. "Okay, maybe

a C-minus," he added, making it sound as if he were able to work Mrs. Dembinski's grading system with surgical precision. "Then with the next one I'll get you into the high Cs. After that a B-minus won't seem so weird. Then I'll have you coast along with B-pluses for a few months before I turn in your first A."

Nelson was now nodding with a grin of his own. Billy's straight-faced delivery had left little doubt that his proposal was meant to be taken seriously.

"Clikkmaster," said Nelson. "You are the man with the plan. You hear that?" he said, turning to Jake. "He's gonna start writing *all* your papers. All of 'em!"

"Maybe I was wrong about you, dude," said Jake to Billy, folding his arms like a Mafia boss granting a promotion to one of his underlings. "You're all right."

"Deal?" said Billy, extending his right hand.

"You kidding?" said Jake, laughing and throwing a can-you-believe-this-guy glance at Nelson. "Deal," Jake said, and slapped his hand into Billy's.

Billy closed his fingers around Jake's and smiled, shaking his hand slowly and firmly. He closed his fingers more firmly still and kept shaking. The handshake went on and on.

"All right, dude," said Jake with a pained smile. "You got a strong handshake. I get the idea."

Billy closed his fingers even more tightly around Jake's. Several months of AFMEC hand-to-hand-combat training had given Billy a formidable grip.

"Dude," said Jake, trying to pull his hand out of Billy's. It was impossible. "Let go of my hand." Jake was trying to sound tough, but a hint of pleading had come into his voice.

"Have to seal the deal, Jake," said Billy, tightening his grip yet further. "We're talking about a very long relationship here, you and me." Billy's eyes locked onto Jake's. "An *understanding*."

Jake dropped the loose-leaf on the ground. Nelson stood

slack-jawed and speechless, amazed by the sight of someone standing up to Jake for what was probably the first time ever.

"So tell me, Jake," said Billy, speaking with the offhandedness of someone who could stay like this all day if necessary. "How soon do you need me to rewrite that paper for you?"

Jake paused to weigh his options, then mumbled, "Forget it. Forget about the paper, man."

"Are you sure, Jake?" Billy relaxed his grip ever so slightly. He sensed his message was now coming through, loud and clear.

"Yeah," said Jake, allowing his fist to open and grow limp.

All at once Billy released his grip altogether. Jake rubbed furiously at his red and pink right hand. Billy leaned down, picked up Jake's paper, and handed it to him. "You dropped this."

"Thanks," said Jake, now unable to look Billy in the eye for anything but the briefest of glances. "Come on, Nel. Let's get out of here."

Billy watched as Nelson and Jake slouched off down the street. He then jumped on his skateboard and sailed off to Marvy Marv's.

The following Saturday, Ana and Billy, along with Billy's parents and Orzamo, hopped an AFMEC-sponsored flight to Guatemala, where they were treated to a lovely afternoon meal at the García family home in the seaside town of Champerico. It was a glorious sunny day, hot and dry with a nice steady breeze blowing through the palm trees. Ana's father put on a Ricardo Ajorna CD, and Ana's mother made a sumptuous meal of arroz con pollo chapina, which turned out to be chicken with rice, olives, capers, and a whole bunch of other mouthwateringly good stuff.

"Tasty," said Ana, "isn't it?" She and Billy were seated on folding chairs on the patio, eating off colorful ceramic plates, while their parents ate and chatted indoors. Orzamo lazed beside them in the shade of a papaya tree.

"Delicioso," said Billy, his mouth half full of rice. "A few more days here and I really *would* start to pack on the pounds."

"Me too," said Ana with a grin.

It was strange how much Billy's thoughts about Ana had changed during the past few days. He'd started off wanting never to go on another creatch op with her. Now he found himself wondering if they would get teamed up again.

Bing bong

"That must be our guests," said Ana's father as he rose to answer the front door.

"Guests?" said Billy to Ana. "You didn't say anything about—"

"Heeeey," came the booming sound of a familiar Sicilian accent. "Where's my little bambina?"

Luigi Bonaducci and Mei Jun strolled into the living room. There were hugs and kisses all around, and Ana's father had to turn the music up a little for it to be heard over the boisterous conversations that ensued. Eventually everyone moved out to the patio to eat dessert and watch the sun go down over the Pacific Ocean.

"Hey, Dad," said Billy. "Any chance of another family funeral this week? I've got a math test I'd really like to get out of."

"No dice, wise guy," said Jim Clikk as he finished off his bowl of baked bananas. "You miss that math test and the only funeral you go to will be your own."

Billy smiled. He knew he probably wouldn't get out of school again anytime soon. Still, there were more creatch ops coming, that much was certain. He looked around at his parents, Mr. and Mrs. García, Ana, and Luigi. They were all full-fledged Affys.

Billy knew he had a lot of work to do before he'd be allowed to join their ranks. How long would it take to complete his training and graduate to full Affy status? Three years? Five? There were no guarantees. He might be out of college by the time he finally passed all the tests and got the official thumbs-up from Mr. Vriffnee. His training was bound to be long, hard, and full of setbacks.

He wouldn't trade it for anything, though. Not in a million years.

Find out how Billy became
an Affy-in-training.

CREATCH BATTLER

CHAPTER 1

SKEETER GIG. BACK LATE, DON'T WAIT UP. DINNER'S IN
THE FUDGE. LOVE, MOM & DAD

Billy Clikk read the Post-it again.

"*Fridge.* She meant fridge." Crumpling up the yellow square, Billy chucked it at the garbage can and watched it fly in and then bounce out onto the kitchen floor. It was the third time this week he'd come home from school to find his parents gone, leaving him to heat leftovers in the microwave, do his homework, and put himself to bed. At this point they could just leave a note reading THE USUAL and he'd know exactly what it meant.

There was an upside, though: Billy was now free to kick back and watch his favorite TV show, *Truly Twisted.* He dashed into the living room, leaped over the couch, grabbed the remote, and switched on the TV.

Truly Twisted was the one program his parents said he must never, never watch. These guys took extreme sports to a whole new level: they once snuck into a church, climbed up the steeple, and bungee-jumped right into the middle of some guy's wedding. It was pretty awesome.

When Billy got to the channel where *Truly Twisted* was supposed to be airing, though, there was nothing more extreme than some lame college tennis championship. "Oh, come on!" Billy cried. They'd bumped the best show on cable for a couple of scrawny guys knocking a ball back and forth.

Billy shut off the TV and slouched back into the kitchen. He yanked open the "fudge," pulled out a brown paper bag, and peeked inside. Cold chicken curry: carryout from the Delhi Deli, an Indian restaurant down the street. Billy used to like their chicken curry. Back before he'd eaten it once or twice a week, every week, for about three years.

Billy pursed his lips, made a farting sound, and tossed the bag back in the refrigerator. He slammed the door a lot harder than he really needed to and stared at the floor. There, next to his foot, sat the crumpled-up Post-it note.

"Are pest problems getting *you* down?" he said, suddenly doing a superdeep TV-commercial voice. "Then you should pick up that phone and call Jim and Linda Clikk, founders of BUGZ-B-GON, the best extermination service in all of Piffling,

Indiana." He leaned down and picked up the wadded note, and as he straightened up, he added a tone of mystery to his voice. The TV commercial had turned into a piece of investigative journalism. "What makes the Clikks so busy? What drives them to spend their every waking hour on extermination jobs— 'skeeter gigs,' as they call them? Is it *really* necessary for them to devote so much of their time and energy to saving total strangers from termites and hornets' nests? Is it just for the money, or is killing bugs some kind of a weird power trip?"

Billy took aim with the Post-it and had another shot at the garbage can. This time the note went in and stayed in.

That's more like it.

Billy changed his posture and pivoted on one foot, transforming himself once again into a reporter.

"And what of Jim and Linda's son, Billy? How does *he* feel about all this?" Billy went on, clutching an imaginary microphone as he strode from the kitchen back to the living room. "Well, let's ask him. Billy, how *do* you feel about all this?"

"You want the truth?" said Billy, switching to his own voice. "I think it stinks. I think it's a lousy way to treat a devoted son who is so bright, well behaved, and good-looking."

Billy drew his eyebrows into an expression of great sympathy: he was the reporter again. "Tell me, Billy, do you think it *bothers* your parents that you have to spend so many evenings at home by yourself? Do you think they feel the least bit *guilty* that you have to eat takeout night after night rather than home-cooked meals? Indeed, do you suppose—as your parents dash madly from one skeeter gig to another—that they even *think* of you *at all*?"

Billy stopped, stood between the couch and the coffee table, and let out a long sigh. He dropped the imaginary microphone and the phony voice along with it.

"I don't know." Billy flopped onto the couch. "Probably not."

It hadn't been so bad the previous year, when Billy's best friend, Nathan Burns, was still living in Piffling. Nathan was the only kid at Piffling Elementary who was as obsessed with extreme sports as Billy was. They used to spend practically every weekend together, mountain-biking the cliffs that led down to the Piffling River, skateboarding across every handrail in town (they both had the scrapes, bruises, and occasional fractures to prove it), and even street luging on their homemade luges, which was apparently outlawed by some city ordinance or another. The only thing Billy and Nathan hadn't tried was sneaking a ride on the brand-new Harley-Davidson Nathan's father had stashed away in the garage.

They would have tried it eventually, for sure. But then Nathan's family moved to Los Angeles for his father's work. There were other kids at Piffling Elementary who were into extreme sports a little. They just weren't willing to risk life and limb the way Nathan was. Billy soon realized that finding a new best friend was going to take a while. In the meantime, it was looking like it would be THE USUAL for many months to come.

Piker, Billy's Scottish terrier, lifted her head from the recliner on the other side of the room, snorted, and went back to sleep.

BACK LATE, DON'T WAIT UP.

Billy had never been able to figure out why so much of his parents' work was done at night. Exterminators didn't normally work at night, did they? Were they trying to catch the bugs snoozing? Kids at school thought he was lucky. "If my parents left *me* alone at night like that," Nelson Skubblemeyer had said just the other day, "I'd be partyin' like nobody's business. I'd be, like, 'Yo, party tonight at my place. . . .' " (Nelson always said the word *party* as if it rhymed with *sauté*: in spite of his name, he'd somehow convinced himself he was the coolest kid in the sixth grade.)

Billy had never thrown a party while his parents were out on a skeeter gig. He wouldn't have been able to get away with it even if he'd tried. There was someone keeping an eye on him.

DRRIIIIIIINGG

Leo Krebs, thought Billy. *Right on schedule.* Billy normally didn't let the phone ring more than twice before answering. But when he was pretty sure it was Leo, the high school sophomore down the street who "looked after" him whenever his parents were gone at night, he had a policy of screening calls.

DRRIIIIIINGG

Billy leaned back into the couch and did his best Leo impersonation: "Dude. Pick up. I know you're there." Doing a good Leo meant breathing a lot of air into your voice and ending every sentence as if it were a question. Like Keanu Reeves, only more so.

DRRIIIIIINGG

Billy's voice had begun to change the previous summer, greatly increasing the range of impersonations he could do (which had been pretty impressive to begin with). "Duu-ude. You're wastin' my time here."

DRRIIIIIINGG

One more ring and the answering machine would kick in.

DRRIIIIIINGG

There was a *plick,* then a *jrrrr,* then: "Your pest problems are at an end . . . ," Jim Clikk's voice said. Billy jumped in and recited the words right along with the answering machine, creating the effect of two Jim Clikks speaking simultaneously. ". . . because you're seconds away from making an appointment with the extermination experts at BUGZ-B-GON. Just leave your name and number after the tone and we'll get back to you as soon as we can."

DWEEEEEP

"Dude." It was Leo, all right. "Pick up. I know you're there."

Billy grabbed the remote off the coffee table and clicked the television on. When dealing with one of Leo's check-in calls, it was essential to have every bit of audiovisual distraction available.

"Duu-ude. You're wastin' my time here."

Billy reached over, grabbed the cordless phone from one of the side tables, and pressed Talk.

"Leonard," he said, knowing how much Leo disliked being called by his full name. Well, at least he *hoped* Leo disliked it. Billy didn't exactly hate Leo, but he wasn't too crazy about him either. Part of it was Leo's *I'm older than you and don't forget it* attitude. Most of it, though, was Billy resenting the whole idea of being baby-sat at all. He was old enough to take care of himself.

"Dude," said Leo in return. He never called Billy anything other than dude. Leo probably called little old ladies dude. "Look, your folks told me they wouldn't be back until, like, midnight or whatever . . ."

Billy was remoting his way through a bunch of cartoon shows. He paused on an old low-budget monster movie.

". . . so I can either come over there and babysit you for a couple hours—which neither of us wants—or just check in again at ten and make sure you're still alive. Not that I want you to be."

"C'mon, Leonard. You don't want anything bad to happen to me. You'd be out twenty bucks a week."

Normally Billy would have come up with a better verbal jab than the twenty bucks line, but he was devoting most of his attention to the image on the television screen: an enormous creature with lobster claws going to great lengths to stomp his way into a cheap imitation of Disneyland. There didn't seem to be any special reason why. Maybe he'd run out of office buildings and power stations to wreck.

"All right, dude. Ten o'clock it is. Pick up the phone next time, will ya?"

"Okay, Leonard. And hey: tell your skater buddies to learn some new moves. My gramma can do better kickflips than that."

Billy shut off the phone with great relief. He knew that the money his parents paid Leo involved him physically being inside the Clikk home. Periodically Leo would skip the phone call and just arrive at the front door. On these occasions he always left behind some very clear proof that he'd been there—doodles on a notepad, a half-finished bottle of Gatorade—apparently thinking a bit of Leo-was-here evidence every once in a while would be enough to convince Billy's parents they weren't completely wasting their twenty dollars.

Doodles on notepads. Bottles of Gatorade. Billy noticed stuff like that: details. He'd always had a knack for it, even when he was just a kindergartner. If the dark blue crayon in Crayola's big box went from being called cerulean one year to cornflower the next, Billy knew about it and had a preference. And it wasn't just kid stuff. If Billy got even half a second's glance under the hood of a Hummer H2, he could tell which parts were new, which were old, and which parts the shady repairman had used strictly to skim money off the bill.

The lobster creature had reached the roller-coaster mountain in the middle of the amusement park and was tearing apart its papier-mâché walls. Sweaty actors with loosened neckties pointed and screamed convincingly.

Man. This is one stupid movie. If I were fighting a monster like that, I'd just pull the zipper on his back, stick my head inside, and tell him to get a better costume.

Billy punched the remote and jumped from channel 63 to 64. The Shopping Network: two middle-aged women going nuts over a very ugly piece of jewelry. Punch, punch, punch, punch: 65, 66, 67, 68. Boring, boring, boring, and boring. He was just about to shut the television off.

Huh?

That guy on TV.

That guy looked an *awful* lot like his dad.

Billy sat up and leaned halfway over the coffee table, staring with all his might. Piker sat up too.

The TV screen was filled with unsteady handheld video: some kind of ticker-tape parade. Street signs in a foreign language, early-morning sunlight. Dark-haired people with open-necked shirts, shouting, cheering. And there, in a big convertible sailing slowly through the crowds . . .

That's Dad!

No, it can't be.

Billy pressed the VCR button on the remote and then hit Record.

Bee-beep, bee-beep, bee-beep

"No tape!" Billy jumped off the couch, leaped over the coffee table, and fumbled for a blank videotape from the shelf under the TV, all the while keeping his eyes glued to the screen. Piker jumped down from the chair and began whining loudly.

"That can't be him," said Billy. "It's impossible."

Billy's heart was beating faster. He tore the cellophane off the videotape and crammed it into the VCR as quickly as he could. He punched the Record button and sat down on the coffee table to continue watching the program.

"That's not Dad. It just . . . can't be. This stuff was obviously shot in a foreign country. Dad never goes to other countries. Except, like, Canada."

But the man had the same face as Billy's father: the wide forehead, the slightly grayed wavy hair, the enormous protruding jaw. There was a woman seated next to him. It was hard to tell because she was wearing a wide-brimmed hat, but that was . . . Billy's mom, wasn't it? She had the same perky nose, the same thin-lipped mouth, and—from what he could see, anyway—was wearing the exact same style of thick-rimmed glasses.

No. Way.

Billy was now leaning so far forward that his face was no more than ten inches from the TV screen. He noticed something about the trees and buildings in the video: everything was dripping with some kind of thick, purplish liquid. As if kids had gone on a rampage with giant purple-yolked eggs.

What the heck is that stuff?

Piker barked once loudly.

A woman's voice accompanied the video, no doubt providing valuable information, but none of it was in English. A small icon in the lower right-hand corner of the TV screen confirmed what Billy already suspected: this was the International Channel, that weird cable station that went from Middle Eastern